## Saul's expression was calm and remote

Then as she came up to him, he smiled; his irresistible charm washed over her like an invigorating flood that renewed her senses.

Candace hesitated, then said with a shy upward glance, "You're being very kind. Thank you."

His hand moved to her elbow as he strode silently beside her. "Castaways are always taken care of in the South Seas. It's a local tradition."

She reacted to the dry note in the deep voice with another doubtful look, but although he was smiling, his eyes were so dazzling that no emotion was discernible. Somewhere deep inside her a tiny trigger set off an alarm. His fingers at her elbow felt like fetters instead of the loose, impersonal grasp of courtesy.

**ROBYN DONALD** lives in northern New Zealand with her husband and children. They love the outdoors and particularly enjoy sailing and stargazing on warm nights. Robyn doesn't remember being taught to read, but rates reading as one of her greatest pleasures, if not a vice. She finds writing intensely rewarding and is continually surprised by the way her characters develop independent lives of their own.

## Books by Robyn Donald

Don't miss any of our special offers. Write to us at the following address for information on our newest releases.

Harlequin Reader Service
P.O. Box 1397, Buffalo, NY 14240
Canadian address: P.O. Box 603,
Fort Erie, Ont. L2A 5X3

# ROBYN DONALD

## the darker side of paradise

**Harlequin Books**

TORONTO • NEW YORK • LONDON
AMSTERDAM • PARIS • SYDNEY • HAMBURG
STOCKHOLM • ATHENS • TOKYO • MILAN

For Averill, Diane, Cavell and Megan,
who know that life without sisters
would be bread without salt,
coffee without caffeine,
champagne without bubbles
and night without the moon.

And for Sally,
because sisters-in-law
are as good as the real thing.

Harlequin Presents first edition July 1991
ISBN 0-373-11376-5

Original hardcover edition published in 1990
by Mills & Boon Limited

THE DARKER SIDE OF PARADISE

# CHAPTER ONE

IN SPITE of the fact that she had come all the way to the South Pacific island of Fala'isi to find him, Candace Hume didn't recognise Saul Jerrard at first sight.

Oh, like almost everyone in the opulent room she turned her head at the first subdued stir at the door of the hotel restaurant, and something in her heart jumped when she caught a glimpse of him as he was being respectfully ushered in. Tall and dark, with the smooth waves of his hair gleaming almost black in the subdued lights, he was formally elegant in the tropical kit of white dinner-jacket and red cummerbund. Candace's eyes lingered on the wide shoulders and long lean legs, but what compelled her attention was his arrogant air of confidence as he walked towards her across the restaurant floor.

Rich, she thought cynically.

Very rich, as the head waiter moved smoothly but rapidly to greet him—smiling!

And powerful with it. Two men she recognised as Australian politicians got to their feet to greet him in a manner that was subtly deferential. His response was cordial but he was clearly not impressed by their greetings or the aura of power that surrounded them. That could well be because his own was infinitely more impressive.

A man born to rule, she decided idly.

As he came closer she drank in his appearance with an odd intensity. Perhaps her thoughts were spearing across the air-conditioned restaurant because he turned his head to look directly at her, and it was then that recognition hit her with an impact that was almost physical.

Although the ritual of greeting was over, a trace of his smile still lingered on his well-cut mouth. It was oddly remote, as though he had no warmth in him at all. His features were striking, so impressive that his looks were not important beyond an austerely magnificent bone-structure.

Toying with the glass of fruit salad that had been all she could afford for dessert, Candace had thought she was being discreet in her fascinated survey, but his brilliant eyes, the rare clear cornflower-blue of the most precious sapphires, sharpened as they met hers. Magician's eyes, shaman's eyes, cold and crystalline, very hard, very keen, fierce as a raptor's predatory gaze, they seemed to pierce right through her outward defences to dissect the vulnerable woman who hid her most intimate thoughts and emotions behind a shield of brisk common sense.

For a second, too brief to be conclusive, she thought he might be going to stop. However, if his lean legs had faltered in their stride, his reflexes were as swift as the eagle's she compared him to. His face hardened; he gave Candace one more piercing, oddly impersonal glance and went on past.

The woman on his arm said something. Sickly Candace realised that she had entirely ignored the fact that he was accompanied. With an involuntary gasp her gaze flew to the beautiful countenance of his companion, then her lashes sank down and a chilling disappointment leached the colour from her face. The woman was at least twenty-five, too old to be Stephanie Jerrard. Was Saul Jerrard's sister not convalescing here on Fala'isi after all?

With averted face she watched as they walked to a table discreetly hidden from the *hoi polloi* by a bank of exotic foliage. The woman on his arm swayed with the conventional model's saunter, but he had the sleek, easy, noiseless gait of a hunter. Into Candace's mind flashed visions of hot, steamy jungles and darkness and death, primitive excitement and desire beyond understanding.

Which was ridiculous. In spite of the cutting chill of those amazing eyes Saul Jerrard was a sophisticated man of the world who confined his predatory instincts to the boardroom. And bedroom, she thought, hiding her febrile excitement with a flippancy she had come to use as a cover for her deepest feelings. For all his wealth and power and discretion, there had been plenty of items in the gossip columns, carefully phrased but easy enough to decipher, and she had devoured them as well as the more mundane articles in the financial Press.

Colour fled her skin, leaving only the clear pale gold of her tan. She blinked ferociously as the tropical palms between them blurred into a hazy veiling. Then he sat down, and the breath in her lungs passed softly between her lips in an explosive little puff.

The mixture of papaw and pineapple, passion-fruit and custard-apple, decorated with the exquisite silken blossom of a hibiscus the colour of a tropical shell, tasted like cotton wool. Keeping her head down, afflicted with the panic-stricken and utterly stupid conviction that in that one searing glance he had seen through the tourist disguise to her hidden reason for being on the island, she managed to force the cool fruit down. She was, she thought grimly, going to pay enough for it! Sheer thrift, engendered by a life when every cent was saved for a specific purpose, insisted that she eat it all.

When it was gone the waiter came over on large sandalled feet and, with the warm smile that she had come to expect from all of the islanders, asked her if she wanted coffee.

'No, thank you,' she said, smiling in return.

He bowed. 'Is there anything else I can get for you?'

Candace said, 'No, that was lovely, thank you. I'll have my bill now, if I may.'

He gave her a somewhat surprised look. 'The cabaret will be on later. It's very good.'

'No, thank you,' she said again.

He leaned a little forward. 'Lots of young men come without partners, ma'am,' he said confidentially. 'When the dancing starts it's very friendly, very informal.'

She was not offended. Although she had only been in Fala'isi a day, she had already found out that one of the qualities which made the Polynesian people who lived there so likeable was their open, honest sensuality.

A far cry from her own attitude, classified by various frustrated men as frigidity. She preferred to call it fastidiousness, while recognising that it was more. Put simply, she was afraid of giving herself wholly. Almost certainly it was caused by the trauma she had associated with love and sex since she had been old enough to understand why her adoptive parents' marriage had broken up. Her father had met someone he fell in love with, completely, abjectly, without any conditions.

She could remember her mother's tears, the confusion and pain and fights. Then, for a while it had been just the two of them on their own, struggling along.

But her mother was not a woman who could manage by herself, and soon she too had found another partner. Unfortunately he did not want her withdrawn daughter, whose fear and anger gave rise to flashes of a ferocious temper. He had his own children, and, as Candace had overheard him say, 'Well, it will make life a lot easier if she goes. She doesn't get on with my two, and, after all, it's not as though she's really yours, is it?'

It still hurt, but not as much as her pretty, weak mother's capitulation. So at the age of ten a bereft, bitterly resentful Candace had been sent to a foster home, categorised as unmanageable. It was then that she'd made the decision never to allow herself to love again. Love, from her small experience of it, was a force that destroyed and broke lives.

Sometimes she wondered if she was ever going to meet a man who could persuade her that the rewards were worth the fear and the possibility of rejection. As she hadn't met one yet, the answer was probably no. So now she smiled at the waiter and said cheerfully, 'It sounds fun, but tonight I want an early night.'

'Certainly, ma'am.'

While he padded silently away she sneaked another look through the thicket of ferns. The red-headed woman was talking, utterly absorbed in the man opposite. Beautiful, with sleepy sensual eyes, a full, red mouth, and exquisite skin as smooth and matt as crêpe, she wore a pale pink dress with great panache. It was obvious that she was accustomed to—and enjoyed—public attention. In that triumphal progress across the floor, hand resting lightly on Saul Jerrard's white sleeve, her eyes had gleamed with an arrogant satisfaction.

As Candace's gaze slid from the exquisite face, her stomach gave an odd lurch. Whether it was coincidence or not, Saul Jerrard was watching her, his expression detached and impassive, but something behind the heavy lids warned her that he would not forget her face. It felt as though he were skewering her soul. She looked away hastily; it took all of her will-power to wait for the bill, and when at last she left it was with an uneasy sensation between her shoulder-blades.

Fala'isi was perfectly safe at night, the streets well-lit, the people of the island uniformly courteous, with a warm, calm pride in themselves and their island that compelled respect, so she had no fears about walking the few blocks back to her motel.

'The closest place to paradise,' the tourist brochures brayed, and for once Candace agreed with the publicity. The island was heartbreakingly beautiful, a superb blend of the stunning natural beauty for which south Pacific islands were justly famed, and a not too frenetic sophistication. Extinct volcanoes formed the high spine

of the island, and a circling coral reef enclosed a lagoon
the colour of emeralds and amethysts and sapphires, in
some places just thrusting through the warm pellucid
waters in a necklace of tiny islands, where coconut palms
inclined their fringed heads towards sparkling beaches.

And the trade winds sighed in each day, cooling the
drowsy fragrant air, whispering in the fronds of the palms
and ruffling the huge flowers of the hibiscus that grew
wild on the roadsides, wafting the erotic sensuous perfume of frangipani and gardenias and ylang-ylang, the
jewels of the tropics, towards the amiable, exotic passers-
by.

Yes, Fala'isi was beautiful beyond all her imaginings.
It was a pity she couldn't enjoy it properly.

Back at the motel she collected her key from the receptionist, smiling ironically at the contrast. Not that
the motel was squalid; unlike most tropical ports, nothing
in Fala'isi could be termed seedy, but it was definitely
budget accommodation, while the hotel had been one
of a worldwide chain noted for their excellence. The sort
of place where you would be bound to find billionaires
like Saul Jerrard and their mistresses. And their sisters.

Trepidation sat heavily in Candace's stomach. She did
not relish danger for its own sake, and that long enigmatic look from Saul Jerrard convinced her that the
quest she had embarked on with such single-minded determination three years ago had more than a few el-
ements of peril.

It had seemed comparatively easy when he was just a
name in the business columns, a grainy picture in the
newspaper. Oh, she had known that her intrusion into
his life was not going to be welcome, but she hadn't realised just how *unapproachable* he would be. Perhaps
Stephanie was like that too, although it seemed unlikely
that a girl of sixteen would have developed that fine line
in unspoken intimidation.

'Oh, hell,' she said, and collapsed on to the bed. Her foster mother had been convinced that swearing was the first step on the way to eternal damnation, and she still enjoyed the small forbidden thrill. Savouring it, she repeated, 'Hell and damnation! The man is just too much.'

Her pleasant low voice with its slight New Zealand accent fell rather too loudly into the humid air. She got up and switched on the ceiling fan. No doubt Saul Jerrard was accustomed to air-conditioning, but the fan worked quite well most of the time. During the day, when she'd realised that it was merely moving the hot air around, she had crossed the road to the beach and spent the long midday hours lying on the coarse white coral sand in the shade of the coconut palms, her busy mind working out schemes to get closer to Saul and Stephanie Jerrard.

Confronted now by the reality of the situation, she winced at an unnerving cramp in her stomach. He had the look of a man capable of protecting his own. Recollections of his power, his hard, uncompromising reputation, his name for unsparing fairness, an article that had described admiringly his 'nice sense of the fitness of revenge', now made her shiver. Seeing him in the flesh had brought the words vividly, frighteningly to life.

She had the ominous suspicion that he wouldn't look at all tolerantly on a strange woman's striking up an acquaintanceship with his sister. However, that, she decided, as she wooed sleep, was just what she was going to do. She had come a long way for that, both in time and distance, too far to retreat now with her mission unaccomplished.

And she had known all about the Jerrards before she set off on this last part of her quest. She had made it her business to discover as much about the family as she could. Much of what she had learned was frankly intimidating; in spite of the family's dislike of publicity there was quite a lot of information to be garnered. She knew that Saul Jerrard had some family connection with another very rich man, Grant Chapman, who lived on Fala'isi, which explained why the Jerrards had a holiday house on the coast a few miles south of the town.

And she knew that Stephanie Jerrard had suffered a bout of glandular fever, and was on the island to convalesce.

She knew both parents were dead. That was one thing she and the Jerrards had in common, she thought cynically. Parents with no staying power. The older Jerrards had died together in an accident six years ago, when Saul was twenty-seven and his sister ten.

Saul had been left in charge of one of the biggest conglomerates in the world, fought an internecine battle still spoken of in awed tones for its bloody savagery, and emerged triumphant, the undisputed master of his inheritance.

No doubt, that financial warfare had hardened the man. Oh, stop thinking of him, she told herself crossly. Think of his sister, instead. Think of a bright, laughing girl with grey eyes and warm blonde hair...

But as Candace lay listening to the distant boom of the rollers on the barrier reef it was not Stephanie Jerrard she imagined. Saul filled her mind, and when at last she slept it was he who chased her through a forest dark as night, rustling with hidden, dangerous life, and finally woke her with his heavy hand on her shoulder.

Dawn's pale light seeped through the curtains as she lay clammy with panic, her heart pounding. For long moments she dragged her breath into her lungs, still in thrall to the fear and the forbidden, primal anticipation. It was hazardous to recall the exact colour of those eyes, the austerely striking bone-structure with the sweep of aquiline nose and the ruthless jut of jaw, the potent male lines of narrow hip, and tautly muscled thigh, and wide shoulder.

When her customary common sense had had time to assert itself she gave a disgusted snort. In spite of his money and the power that clung to him like a tangible aura, Saul Jerrard was only a man. OK, so the sheer impact of his personality was enough to set you back on your heels, but that was probably what growing up with a billion dollars for an inheritance did to a man. Whatever, it was childish and cowardly to turn him into a nightmare!

Rising, she went into the small bathroom, stripped off her thin cotton nightshirt and stood for a moment, trying to decide whether to swim or shower. Scented with frangipani and an evocative hint of coconut and spices, the air smoothed itself over her body. Her skin tightened. Saul Jerrard gate-crashed her thoughts again; she saw him, lean and darkly dangerous with a male magnetism that had crackled right around the big dining-room like summer lightning.

No doubt he had spent that night with the redheaded woman. What was he like as a lover? Superb, she thought hollowly. He had that air of physical assurance, as though whatever he did was carried through with flair and intelligence and subtlety.

Involuntarily she looked down at her own body. She knew that her main attraction was her hair, amber with streaks of gold to lighten it, curling just over the lobes of her ears. She wasn't sleek, not like the red-headed woman, who was tall but had fragile bones and delicate wrists and ankles.

Candace's brows met as she assessed breasts which were just a bit too ample, hips that made a cradle too earthy for sophistication. The redhead was tanned, whereas she had to be careful; the best her skin would do was wild honey, clear and pale gold. And the redhead was beautiful in a pampered, exotic way, whereas Candace Hume had little to recommend her beyond good skin and a certain regularity of features. Transparent grey

eyes were not as exciting as green-gold, and her mouth
was not fashionably wide. Oh, it curled up at the corners,
and her bottom lip was a little plumper than the top but
there was none of the sensuality of the other woman's
smile.

With an exclamation of disgust she began to slide into
her bathing suit. What did it matter what she looked
like? She had no intention of competing for a man's
favours.

Outside it was as cool as it was ever going to be on
Fala'isi, which meant that the air was balmy and fresh,
with little of the humidity that marked the afternoon
hours. The radiant sky had already assumed the deep
blue of the tropics and the waters of the lagoon faceted
the sun's rays into golden shafts of light. A dove called,
and was answered by the liquid warbling of another bird.
Early as it was, there were people about, golden-brown
islanders with their bright cool clothing and erect graceful
walk and warm slow smiles.

By the time she had walked across the road and down
the beach she too was smiling, her night terrors gone
into the limbo from which they had come. Saul Jerrard
was no doubt a hard man, but if she was careful he
wouldn't know what her plans were until it was too late
for him to do anything about them.

However, first of all she was going to have to find out
where Stephanie lived, and what she was likely to be
doing. A comment from the receptionist as she collected
her key after her swim gave her an idea.

'You going to the market today?' she asked.

Candace said, 'I thought it was held earlier in the
morning.'

'Oh, if you want to buy food, yes, that's right, you
get the best stuff just after sunrise. But today is the day
they sell the handicrafts.' She grinned. 'Some lovely work
there. Shell beadwork, basketry, sennit—all the ladies
like to go to the market today. Even the cruise ships try

to get in on a Wednesday for the handicraft market. Great souvenirs, really good stuff, and not too dear, although you pay a lot for the best. If you go, have a look at the strings of pearls. Oh,' at Candace's arched brows, 'not the real black pearls; these are made from the shells they throw away, and they're really pretty. And a lot cheaper than the real thing!'

Possibly Stephanie liked buying souvenirs. In which case, the market was the logical place for her to be. It was worth a try, anyway. And if she didn't turn up, Candace told herself firmly, well, she would be content with just wandering through, eyeing the throng of shoppers and tourists.

The market, a large open area down by the docks with open sheds around the edge, was crammed with holiday-makers exclaiming over the incredible array of wares, revelling in the different, exotic, richly mingled sights and sounds. Firmly squashing the vagrant realisation that everyone there seemed to have a companion, she found herself a vantage-point beside a stall, and let her eyes rove the crowds. Isolation was nothing new to her; in one way or another she had been alone all her life. She accepted it, enjoyed it, had even in some strange way come to rely on it.

The receptionist had been right in her description of the crafts, especially the exquisite beaded work. Candace looked longingly at the strings of tiny iridescent beads carved from oyster shells. She sighed a little. They were costly, although not in the same league as the magnificent black pearls displayed in one or two of the up-market jewellers' shops in the main street. Fala'isi's fabled black pearls, so enormously expensive that no prices had been shown, had glowed with a deep inner light, smooth, the subtle sheen almost tactile. She had been awestruck at their superb lustre, in shades ranging from the grey of dawn to the depths of midnight.

However, the beaded jewellery was superb, and she was admiring it and wondering how on earth anyone would have such patience, when her eyes were snagged by a blazing crown of hair a few feet away.

The red-headed woman turned, said something to someone behind her, out of Candace's sight. Instantly alert, she craned her neck. Another woman stepped into view, a thin, tall girl with hair the colour of rusty leaves in autumn. Candace's heart gave a great lurch of excitement as she took an impulsive step forward.

Then she saw the man with them. An islander, big and burly, dressed in the same bright casual clothes of his compatriots, but his penetrating gaze continually swept the crowd. He was, she realised with a cold feeling in the pit of her stomach, a bodyguard.

She fought down the irrational impulse to step back and slowly ease out of sight. Elaborately casual, she let her eyes move to the tall girl who was frowning down at her companion. Her throat closed convulsively. Excitement and a great triumph surged through her. It had to be Stephanie Jerrard. Candace's reaction was so extreme that for a second she thought she might burst into tears. Biting her lips so hard that a bead of blood tasted salt on her tongue, she fought for control.

A tout came through the crowd, a multitude of garlands looping his neck in a swathe of silken colour and scent, and beseeched the pair of women to buy one, thrusting the fragrant clusters towards them as he went into his spiel. The red-headed woman frowned as the bodyguard said something soft and succinct. The flower-seller backed off with such speed that Candace might have been amused if she hadn't been so shaken.

The girl she had come so far to find turned her head; she was smiling, obviously amused by the abrupt departure of the garland-seller, her gaze roving idly across the jostling, happy crowd, and as she turned her head

Candace met eyes the cornflower colour of Saul Jerrard's, brilliant with laughter.

Not a compassionate little sister, she thought, and then, habitually cynical, but a Jerrard doesn't have to be compassionate. After all, cushioned by wealth, why should she care how the peasants live?

Through lowered lashes she watched avidly as the group walked through the crowd. By moving inconspicuously, she managed to arrive at a stall at the same time as they did. Her heart was hammering in her breast so loudly that she couldn't hear their voices, and the sophisticated, intricate patterns of the shell beads danced jaggedly in front of her eyes.

Swallowing, she shook her head at the eager importunities of the stallkeeper and stood back, ostensibly to let the Jerrard party move closer to the front of the booth. Her eyes lingered compulsively on the profile of the girl in front of her. Stephanie slanted her a warm smile of thanks and a nod, and she rather thought her heart-strings might snap at the irony of it.

'That's what I want,' Stephanie Jerrard said in a clear voice, pointing to a superb plaited string of shell 'pearls'.

Candace winced, for the clipped English accent was like a blow, emphasising starkly the distance that separated them.

Lifting bored eyebrows, the red-headed woman made no attempt to modulate her voice. 'Why waste time on these? Oh, they're pretty, and the workmanship is exquisite, but why don't you buy some black pearls as a souvenir?'

The girl gave her a tolerant look. 'Saul does not approve of expensive jewellery on young girls.'

'Well, can't you persuade him?' There was a note of what—envy? greed?—in the cool voice.

Stephanie Jerrard's brilliant eyes rested on her companion's lovely face with something like scorn, quickly hidden. In a very dry voice she said, 'He's not very amenable to persuasion from me, I'm afraid. *You* could always try; he might be more likely to listen to you.'

The red-headed woman flushed, and sent her an unpleasant look, instantly suppressed. Stephanie gave an odd little shrug and turned back to the shell beads.

A worldly, sophisticated Jerrard, this one. Perhaps it was inevitable, growing up in circles of privilege and wealth.

The redhead recovered her poise and gave a delicious gurgle of laughter. 'Steph, you know very well your brother's not amenable to anyone's persuasion. He goes his own way, does his own thing, and is about as easy to coax as a granite wall.'

Steph! It was strange to hear confirmation of all her hopes, all her aspirations and aims and ambitions, come in a casual remark.

Candace's breath stopped in her throat; she made an odd little noise. Then she looked up to find the bodyguard's eyes on her, suspicious and hard, and in a mixture of panic and agitation she did the only thing she could think of to allay suspicion, and put a hand to her forehead, pretending to be dizzy.

'Put your head between your knees!' The voice came from behind. It was hard and peremptory, the arm about her shoulders supportive.

Without resistance she obeyed, sinking to the ground and resting her head on her knees until she judged enough time had passed to be consistent. Then she looked up, straight into the eyes of Saul Jerrard.

They were so cold. Candace thought of ice, thousands of years old, piercing her heart with its frigid chill; all colour fled from her skin, leaving her white and shaken. Huskily, racked by foolish guilt, desperate to get away from him, she stammered, 'I—it must be the heat. I'll go outside. Thank you.'

'Wait a moment,' he said crisply, his face impassive.

Her eyes darkened in confusion and fell before his glittering scrutiny, coming to rest helplessly on the lean dark fingers, long, elegant yet strong as they moved to make a quick gesture at the bodyguard. He turned and said something to the staring crowd and instantly they began to melt away.

Stephanie Jerrard bent over, her face anxious and concerned. 'You still look awfully pale,' she said. 'Saul, what will we do?'

'Get her out where it's a little cooler.' He answered his sister's anxious enquiry with terse confidence, and as that brilliant gaze captured hers again Candace realised that Saul Jerrard had been born with a compelling authority that youth had not weakened and age would not destroy; dizzily she thought that he dominated every situation by the stamp of his concentrated personality.

His intense gaze hardened. In a curt tone he asked, 'Are you all right? Do you think you could stand now?'

She nodded, pale lips barely stretching in a travesty of a smile. 'I'm terribly sorry, I'll be perfectly all right as soon as I get out of the heat.'

Stephanie Jerrard said sympathetically, 'All of us will, I'm sure. Saul, why don't we take Miss...'

'Hume, but it's all right——'

'...Miss Hume outside into the shade of one of the trees?'

The arm about her shoulder tightened. 'Certainly,' he said smoothly, hiding his lack of enthusiasm with an even voice. 'Miss Hume, there's a café not far away with air-conditioning. Do you think you can make it, or shall I carry you there?'

'No,' she muttered, horrified at the prospect. 'I can make it on my own, thank you.'

'Shall we all go?' the clear, confident young voice of his sister asked. 'I'm hot and sticky myself. I'd love something cool to drink.'

'Why don't we go home?' That was the redhead, her voice petulant and annoyed. 'We can put——'

'Where are you staying, Miss Hume?'

Saul Jerrard's interruption was without emphasis, but as he helped her to her feet she met Stephanie's gaze, wide and still troubled, and smiled reassuringly, hoping she had pulled it off, that no one, especially not the man whose strength was supporting her, realised that the supposed 'faint' had been ninety per cent acting.

'Where are you staying, Miss Hume?' he repeated, his arm steel-strong around her waist.

She felt guilty when she gave the name of her motel and Stephanie said impetuously, 'Oh, good, that's on our way home. We'll drop you off after we've all had a drink to cool down.'

Candace resisted the craven urge to pull herself away, to say that she was perfectly all right, that she could manage. She had been offered a small miracle and she wasn't going to allow cowardice to make her flee. Leaning a little more heavily on the arm around her waist, she felt Saul stiffen.

Disbelief? A swift upwards glance revealed hawk-like features, composed and distant. Nothing to be learned there. A further slanting peep at the guard was just as uncommunicative. If he was suspicious he wasn't showing any signs of it, but she had better proceed on the assumption that he was. It was his job to distrust everyone. She had to allay those fears as best she could.

A few minutes later, safely ensconced in the wonderful coolness of the restaurant, she sipped fresh pineapple juice mixed with icy soda water and felt the colour flow back into her cheeks. The guard appeared to be downing his drink with every appearance of enjoyment, but she could feel his covert survey in every fibre of her being. The red-headed woman had ordered something alcoholic and sat looking at it as though there were a rather nasty smell under her nose. Saul Jerrard was enigmatic, his eyes resting rather too frequently for comfort on Candace's small, neat features as though trying to see what was happening beneath the flushed satin of her skin. Only Stephanie showed any real concern.

'It's awfully hot in the market, isn't it?' she said cheerfully. 'Even the locals fan themselves all the time—had you noticed?'

Candace smiled. 'I had. If I ever brave it again a fan is the first thing I'm going to buy.'

Stephanie's eyes lit up with the fervour of a born-again shopper. 'Try the ones woven from plaited coconut fibre. They're beautiful, and as well as being useful they make a nice souvenir.'

'I'll do that, thank you. Anything else you can recommend for souvenirs?'

'Well, you could try the strings of shell pearls. They're unique to Fala'isi because they're made from the special black oyster-shell. They take ages to do, and I think they're very pretty.'

With a snide little smile the redhead said dulcetly, 'I don't think Miss Hume would want to spend quite so much on a souvenir, Stephie. If I were you, Miss Hume, I'd buy a hat. Then you might not feel the heat quite so much.'

Candace bristled as she saw the ready colour of youth run like wildfire through the younger woman's skin, but she applauded the natural dignity of her response. 'In that case, there are some very good handicrafts in the market, or at Trader Joe's on the main street. Awful name, good shop. It's an excellent idea to go to the museum first so that you can see what they should look like. Unfortunately some of the souvenirs are not of very high standard.'

The other woman gave a delicate little yawn, like a cat. 'Oh, you're a purist, dearest girl. I'm sure the ar-

tistic value is not important—all Miss Hume wants is
something to show that she's been here.'

Candace was unaccustomed to being treated with such
marked contempt, and her teeth met with a tiny snap.
Hurriedly, before she could vocalise the words that came
quivering to her tongue, Stephanie intervened. 'I can't
go on calling you Miss Hume. I'm Stephanie Jerrard,
and this is Lydia Woolcott.' A momentary hesitation and
she added, 'And this is my brother Saul. And Gil.'

Evenly, her New Zealand drawl slow and pleasant,
Candace murmured a general, 'How do you do?'

Lydia looked bored and Saul's narrow stare couldn't
have been less welcoming, but she persevered, wanting
to somehow impress her personality on Stephanie so that
she would be remembered. 'My name's Candace,' she
said pleasantly.

Smiling at the younger woman's quizzical look, she
spelled it out. Stephanie's face cleared. 'Oh, I've seen it
written, but I always thought the last syllable was pronounced "ace", not "iss".'

Candace shrugged. 'That's the way my mother always
said it.'

Not liking the name, but stuck with it as the one
condition of the adoption, her adoptive mother had
shortened it to Candy. When she had arrived at her
foster-home Candace had refused to answer to anything
other than her full name. It had been her only link with
her birth mother.

Saul Jerrard enquired lazily, 'Can I get anyone another
drink? If not, I think it's time we left.'

Lydia moved with such conscious grace that it was
impossible to imagine her hurrying, but she was the first
to her feet.

Obediently Stephanie followed her, but halfway up she
stopped, looking worriedly at Candace, and asked, 'Are
you sure you're ready to go, because if you're
not——?'

Better not push her luck too far. Smiling a little wryly, she too rose. 'No, I'm fine, thank you. I'll go back to my motel and have a good long swim.'

But just in case they left her there, something she was convinced they all, apart from Stephanie, wanted to do, she allowed herself to falter a little as they came out into the blinding glare of the sun.

Saul immediately took her arm, holding it a little too firmly. She thought she could feel his irritation running through his fingertips into her arm, sizzling like small electric shocks through the skin and up her arm, even reaching her heart, but nothing of it showed in his face or his voice. 'Gil, go and get the car. We'll wait in the shade here.'

The two men exchanged looks, then the bodyguard swung off through the crowd. Clearly he was not happy about going. Surely it was unlikely that anyone could do any harm in a crowd like this? Still, perhaps all security men were paranoid.

'Would you like to wait inside?' Saul's voice was cool, almost indolent, but Candace knew better than to trust it. He was like a stalking hunter, blending into the background, waiting for the perfect moment to strike the killing blow.

'No,' she said quickly. 'No, I feel fine, thank you.'

Stephanie grinned and chanted with an amusing little quirk of her brows, 'It's not the heat, you know, it's the humidity. I know what it's like. Whenever I come here I spend the first week panting in the pool.'

Candace laughed. 'I know the feeling.'

'Are you Australian? You don't sound——'

Still intent on establishing some sort of bond, Candace said, 'No, I'm from New Zealand. We sound a little alike, but there is a difference in the accents.'

Stephanie's blue eyes, so frank and friendly, revealed nothing but interest. Did she know that she too had been born in New Zealand? From her lack of response it didn't seem likely. Chuckling, she suggested, 'Like Canadians and Americans?'

Candace smothered a pang of disappointment with wry laughter. 'Exactly the same. Heaven help you if you mistake one for the other.'

'Oh, I know. At school we have——'

Saul interposed easily but with authority, 'Stephanie, could you move aside a little? I think someone is trying to get past.'

Someone was, but Saul's words were clearly a warning, and one his sister heeded. After giving way to a middle-aged couple in identically bilious Hawaiian shirts, she began chatting again, but about generalities this time, suggesting places that Candace could go while she was staying on the island, things to do. Polite nothings.

Candace followed her lead, setting out to make herself amusing and non-threatening. More than anything she wanted to do something, say something that would impress her personality on Stephanie so that later, when she made contact again, she would be remembered.

Unfortunately nothing but platitudes of the most banal kind occurred to her before the car arrived, large and luxurious but not ostentatious.

Once at her motel she had to say her thanks and her goodbyes under the watchful eyes of the others. It took all her spirit and courage to do it with a smile and a voice that didn't waver, but she managed, standing in the shade of the huge banyan tree until the vehicle was out of sight before going into the motel. Blinking, she realised that she knew now what it felt like to be torn apart by the violence of her emotions.

In the sanctuary of her room she bit her lip to keep back the stupid, sudden tears that threatened to spill over. She had done what she wanted to. She had made contact. She had spoken to Stephanie Jerrard. Why then feel as though all purpose had gone from her life?

It was ridiculous. In a way, she told herself stoutly as she walked along the cool open corridor, she could now begin to live, decide what to do with her life. First the drifting years, then the years of searching, all were over now. She had found her pot of gold, the treasure at the end of the rainbow. Now she would make a new start, a good life.

# CHAPTER TWO

THE following two days were spent in limbo. Oh, Candace lay on the beach, she ate, she did some minor sightseeing, and she hovered around the market-place, and the town, waiting for a further glimpse of the Jerrards.

And while she did this she told herself very firmly that she was being an idiot, that she had already accomplished all she had set out to do. She had seen Stephanie, spoken to her, with any luck she had made some impression on her so that when she contacted her again she would be remembered—pleasantly.

The most sensible, pragmatic thing to do was accept that as the sisters of billionaires were very carefully guarded there was almost no likelihood of speaking to her again. That being so, Candace would enjoy the rest of her holiday, then go back home refreshed and ready for another year in the library.

It was with this eminently sensible decision made that she booked a ticket for a lagoon cruise, determined to enjoy herself and forget the presence of the girl she had sought for three years.

Early in the morning, when the waters of the lagoon were still soft grey, she pulled a hat on over her curls and went down to the open bus that was collecting tourists who had booked on the lagoon cruise. They were a cheerful lot, mostly Australians and New Zealanders leavened by a few Americans and some from more exotic countries, all determined to enjoy themselves, and most exuding that careless holiday vivacity that made talking to strangers almost obligatory.

As they embarked on the big white catamaran Candace decided that she had made the right decision. She wasn't going to mope any longer. Fala'isi had a lot to offer, and she was going to sample it. Smiling at a sunburned man whose accent told her he came from Germany, she allowed herself to be beguiled into conversation.

The throbbing engines of the big boat were muffled by the water as it made its way across the glittering lagoon towards the small coral atolls that dotted the border reef. A wind, cooler than it was on land, teased toffee-coloured strands of silk out from beneath her hat, and they stuck slightly to the sunscreen she had rubbed into her cheeks. Her spirits rose. She gave a wide, uncomplicated smile to a small Australian boy with bright yellow zinc ointment slashed like war-paint across his nose and mouth and forehead. Yes, she thought eagerly, she had definitely done the right thing.

They stopped off one of the islands for snorkelling, and a second for shelling, and on a third, beneath the graceful crowns of a plantation of coconut palms, lunched on an exotic South Seas barbecue with fresh-caught fish and an array of delicious, unusual fruits and vegetables. It was highly artificial, but enjoyable for all that. Candace ate with an enthusiastic appetite, lightly flirting with a cheerful man about her age who confided that he came from Melbourne.

On the way back, after they had swum the heat of the afternoon away, the big boat eased closer in to the coast and the guide began to point out landmarks of interest, telling them a little about the frequently bloody, always fascinating history of the island, mixing legends with cold hard facts, tall tales with dark deeds of unabashed savagery.

'Not that you need worry now,' he assured them, his brown face cheerful. 'Fala'isi is one of the most law-abiding places in the South Pacific. We like to lead much more placid lives than our ancestors did!'

Everyone smiled, and one woman asked curiously, 'Whose house is that on the low cliff over there? It has a high thatched roof like a chief's, but it doesn't seem to be in a village.'

The guide looked a little self-conscious. Intrigued, Candace followed his gaze to the big house above its bank of thick, jungly growth. Below, embraced by the blinding half-circle of a small bay, was a large white cruiser, with a tall, spindly erection like a tower rising above the flying bridge.

'Oh, that belongs to one of our important men,' the guide said a little too swiftly.

'It looks lovely,' the woman remarked. 'Right on the edge of the rain forest like that—would we be able to go in there?'

This time the guide looked uncomfortable. 'No, I'm afraid it's private property.' He grinned. 'You set foot on the beach and you might find big dogs and bigger men asking you not too politely what you're doing there. If you want to see the rainforest, ma'am, we have an excellent tour into the mountains in the interior. Take that and you'll see enough jungle to last you a lifetime.'

'I thought there wasn't really any private land on Fala'isi,' the woman persevered in a puzzled tone. 'Don't the islanders enjoy a communal lifestyle, with communally owned land.

'Yes, but there are a few patches that are privately owned. Just a quirk of history. That is one of them.'

A man gave an envious smile. 'I'll bet that's Jerrard's. You know, the billionaire. He's an islander, isn't he? I remember reading somewhere that he and Grant Chapman are cousins.'

'Oh, Mr Chapman is an islander,' the guide said smoothly. 'He's descended from the last surviving princess of the island, and yes, it's true that he and Mr Jerrard are cousins, but Mr Jerrard didn't grow up here.'

'And is that his place?'

The woman again. Candace scanned the pleasant brown face of the guide with an intentness that rendered her eyes silver. Beside her the young man from Melbourne muttered, 'Persistent, isn't she?'

Finally, and with what she sensed was some considerable reluctance, the guide conceded, 'Yes, ma'am, that is his place.'

An idea bounced fullblown into Candace's head.

So startling, so fundamentally shocking was it that she immediately banished it, and spent the rest of the trip back listening to the guide and responding with somewhat absent attention to the conversation of the man from Melbourne.

However, when he suggested they have a drink together, she gave him a slow regretful smile and refused, and had forgotten his face and name by the time she reached the motel.

Back in her bedroom that idea returned to taunt and tempt her. In a straight line, as the fish swam, Saul Jerrard's summer house wasn't very far down the coast. If she somehow got herself stranded on that beach...

Big dogs. And large bodyguards.

A small cold shiver sneaked the length of her spine. Gil Whoever-he-was hadn't struck her as being particularly understanding. He had eyes that were every bit as cold as Saul Jerrard's.

Nevertheless, the dogs wouldn't tear her to bits. Guard dogs weren't allowed to do that. No doubt they had been trained to hold, and keep; she had once seen a television documentary detailing the sort of training guard dogs went through, and instant death for intruders hadn't been part of it.

Besides, she was rather good with animals. Most liked her.

So if she hired one of the small catamarans for the day, say, and then somehow ended up on the beach below the house...

She might, of course, be politely escorted off the place without seeing anyone at all but whatever bodyguards minded it.

On the other hand, she might not.

Into her mind there danced the image of a tall girl with blue eyes and rusty red curls. It was much worse now that she had actually seen her. Anything, she thought with a streak of recklessness she hadn't known she possessed, anything was worth a try if it got her a chance to talk to Stephanie Jerrard again.

As it happened, her plan was almost ridiculously easy to put into action. After lunch the next day she managed to convince the boatman that she knew how to sail and, refusing to take one of the lithe brown islanders with her as crew, she hired the gaily coloured catamaran for an afternoon, promising to have it back by five.

The amount it cost put a fair dint in her spending money, but after all, in spite of what the insufferable Lydia had said, she hadn't come here to spend money on souvenirs. Although much less tangible than strings of shell beads, her mementos were going to be just as evocative of the island, and the occasion. Donning cotton shirt and shorts over her bikini, she smothered every exposed inch of skin with sunscreen, pulled on a peaked cap to protect her nose and lips, and set off.

She had not been lying when she'd claimed to be able to sail. Her high school had run a vigorous elective sailing programme, and she had been good at it, eventually skippering one of the school yachts in races every weekend during the summer. It was, she discovered, the sort of skill that didn't fade. Within minutes she realised that the catamaran was simpler to sail than the school yacht, and her confidence increased when she found it answered sweetly and immediately to her hand on the tiller. Even better, when it came to going about it was slower, thus easier to manage; no jib meant no fuss with sheets, and the warm steady wind sprang no surprises on her.

Buoyed by excitement, her grey eyes sparkling with daredevil anticipation, she sailed back and forth across the lagoon, slowly pulling away from the big resort hotels and the little town. At first she felt ridiculously exposed, almost as though she were under suspicious observation, and had to stop herself from looking over her shoulder; there were plenty of other boats about, of all shapes and sizes, so of course she was quite inconspicuous.

Quite soon the house where Stephanie Jerrard lived appeared on its jungly little bluff, growing very slowly as Candace tacked quietly down the coast. Occasionally she had to get to her feet and check out the seabed ahead, squinting against the bright sea. The water was clear as glass, and although there were clumps of rock most of them were easy enough to see and too far down to be any danger to centreboard or rudder.

One of the tourist boats idled past; she waved to the holiday makers who lined the side, and called a few frivolous replies to their comments, enjoying it when they left her and the deep note of the engines had died away. In spite of the flock of butterflies that had taken up residence in her stomach it was superbly peaceful, but very hot, even though she sat in the shade of the sail.

And then, when at last the sun was beginning to tilt inexorably towards the west, she was there. Casually, as though someone was watching her from the thick vegetation on shore, she went about in the mouth of the little bay. Casually she sailed in, around the cruiser, admired its racy, sweeping lines, the use of immense amounts of money to achieve a lean, pared-down beauty, state of the art.

Then, casually, like the consummate tourist, interested in everything, she turned the sleek twin bows towards the shore.

In the sizzling heat of the afternoon nothing moved, no sign of dog or man, no sign of life at all. The tiny waves lounged listlessly up on to the glaring white sand, darkening it, easing back. Behind the grey arcs of the coconut palms the leaves of the jungle trees hung limply in the sun, masking the ground from her sight, a still, waiting wall composed of a myriad lush greens. Feeling a little like Robinson Crusoe and a mixture of all three boys from *Coral Island*, she stepped into warm, knee-deep water.

Now that she had achieved her aim, she was finally there, a sudden, unwelcome panic held her rigid. Her heartbeat rattled in her ears so noisily that she couldn't hear a sound.

She drew a deep, impeded breath, willing her pulse-rate down, and pushed a lock of caramel hair back from her small face. Trembling fingers snagged in the thick, damp curls; she bit down on to a full, passionate bottom lip and stood for a moment staring up at the tropical forest that clothed the steep face between the beach and the house. A rustle from behind spun her small slender figure around, but no coconut crab advanced along the beach towards her, ferocious claws held menacingly up. Hysteria clogged her throat; with superhuman will-power she controlled it. She had not come this far, risked so much, to throw it all away in unbridled emotion.

Besides, she didn't know whether there were such things as coconut crabs on Fala'isi. It was stupid to lose her nerve over something that might not live within five hundred or so miles. With a brisk mental instruction to take it easy, she pulled at the thin cotton shirt, straightening it.

Now, what would your typical tourist do at this juncture? She would go off the beach and sit for a while in the shade of the trees.

It took a little more effort than she had expected to yank the catamaran up on to the clinging sand, and when she had done it to her satisfaction her temples were unpleasantly wet; using her forearm, she pushed the curls back then lowered the sail to prevent it flapping. Excitement and foreboding proved a potent cocktail, holding her still as her eyes scanned the beach and the dark, still vegetation. No sign of the house was visible from where she stood.

Another rustle, this time from beneath the coconut palms, made her start violently. It came again, and she sank to her knees on the blazing sand, presenting as small and unthreatening a target as she could to the two huge Dobermanns that bounded down from the trees.

It didn't make any difference that she had expected them; her heart still lurched. However, it was vital that she show no fear, so she mastered her emotions. Lean and lethal and dark as sin as these ones were—surely, she thought absurdly, much bigger than normal Dobermanns?—her small frame felt horribly vulnerable as she crouched and waited for them to come up.

As she had anticipated, they were exceptionally well trained. In a businesslike manner they ranged themselves in front of her, not growling, not even particularly threatening. Just waiting, the intelligent eyes keeping her under intent surveillance.

'Hello, chaps,' she said in a soft low voice, even yet filled with colour. 'Having fun?'

One advanced a curious nose and sniffed her delicately. Relaxing, yet alert, she made a few admiring comments on their physical perfection. The nearer one seemed prepared to be lulled into amiability by the soothing witchery of her voice, but the other kept its distance.

'Wise boy,' she murmured. 'Oh, yes, you're a wise one, aren't you?'

But she had lost them. At a slither of sound from up the cliff both dogs looked away, ears pricking. Slowly, Candace turned her head. Like a piece of the dark primeval forest, a man stepped noiselessly from beneath the trees; he stood for a moment, watching her, tall and intimidating and lean, dressed in darkness, yet she could feel the cold speculation in his glance beating against her.

She had expected a minion, a security man, but this was Saul Jerrard himself. A bewildering mixture of emotions dried her mouth and dilated her eyes as she stayed in her submissive posture and watched him walk arrogantly, with a silent grace across the beach. She was horrified to discover that predominant among them was fear.

Of course, she had always known that her quest carried the seeds of danger, that at its end she might find great joy, or shattering sorrow. It was just that it had seemed so much easier back in New Zealand! Her lashes were weighted with recognition and foreboding as he came to a stop a few feet away from her. Danger shimmered around him in an intense aura, glittering, perilous as all quarries of all quests were, beautiful and two-edged.

At that moment, Candace would have given almost anything to be back at home in Auckland.

'This is a private beach,' he said after a tense moment. His voice was deep and cool, the upper-class English clipped and as impersonal as though they had never met before. 'What are you doing here?'

'Being held in custody.' She allowed a note of indignation to sharpen her tone. 'Believe me, Mr Jerrard, I didn't realise that I was likely to be attacked by dogs if I landed here.'

'You knew this was private.' When she hesitated he said smoothly, 'Normally they warn you at the motel not to land here.'

It was a relief to be able to shake her head. 'No, they didn't warn me,' she said.

'But you knew this was my private beach.'

Something in his tone made her flush and raise her indignant eyes to meet his. He thought she was chasing him! It was sheer anger that enabled her to lie with conviction. 'No,' she said firmly.

There was a moment when her nerves screamed with tension, then his heavy lids came down to hide the polished blue of his eyes. 'I see,' he said in a voice so remote that she averted her gaze again. Suddenly realising how incredibly stupid she had been to think that she might have a chance of fooling him, she touched sun-parched lips with a tentative tongue.

The silence stretched out unbearably. His unwavering regard burned over her skin. One of the dogs snorted softly, but, like their master, both kept their eyes fixed on her. A sudden shiver pulled her skin tight.

'You'd better come up to the house.' His voice was indifferent. Why, then, did she get the impression that it was no suggestion he had made, but a command, and that behind the austerely handsome mask of his face his brain was working at top speed?

Quickly, before she had time to change her mind and obey the instincts that were screaming at her to get the hell out of there so fast she'd scorch the water, she said, 'Thank you. If I could, I'd like a drink of water. Then I'll leave you to your privacy.' He said nothing, those strange eyes burning down at her from beneath their heavy lids. She managed a weak smile. 'Can I get up now, or will they eat me if I move?'

White teeth flashed in the teak darkness of his face. 'You can get up, of course. Heel, Joe, heel, Bet.'

Excitement rode high in Candace's veins, relief flooding her with almost physical effect. Chuckling, she said, 'Joe? Bet? What sort of names are those, for heaven's sake? Dogs like these deserve infinitely more interesting names. How about Thor and Brunnhild?'

'Joe and Bet suffice,' he said smoothly, moving closer. 'Here, take my hand.'

It was warm and strong and lean, his strength obvious as he pulled her with a deceptively gentle movement to her feet. 'Thanks. I think my bones must have locked,' she said, grimacing a little as the blood rushed painfully through her legs. Staggering, she clutched at him. He stiffened, and her hands jerked back. Blood rushed painfully to her skin; she shivered, and shot him a quick resentful glance. For heaven's sake, couldn't he see that she had no designs on him, his money or his position?

He was much taller than she, and his height was daunting. Tilting her head back, she judged him to be six feet two or three, with shoulders that were deceptively wide. His spare grace somehow overshadowed his size, so it was with a shock that she realised that her head only came to about halfway up his chest. An odd little sensation trickled down her spine like slow lightning.

She opened her mouth to rush into speech—anything to break the charged silence. Then, like a benediction, came the liquid sweetness of a birdcall, the notes softly dropping into the still, warm air, before rising to a smooth, rolling trill. Swept by delight, Candace listened until the exquisite sounds died away like distant bells across a mountain valley. It was unbearably beautiful, so unexpected that stupid sudden tears magnified her eyes.

'Oh, what is it?' she breathed, as the haunting enchantment of silver notes echoed again through the darkness of the rain forest like an elusive summons to an unknowable, unattainable paradise.

Caught in its spell, they waited in a tableau, the two dogs still as statues behind their master, and he so close to Candace that she could see the cold brilliance of his eyes as they roved her small neat features, irradiated with a kind of rapture.

'What is it?' she whispered again when the last note had faded into nothingness.

His cold English accent was alien on the throbbing air. 'The tikau bird. Uncommon, especially on the coast; its normal range is confined to the mountains. It sings early in the morning and occasionally on moonlit nights. Almost never during the day.' The frozen blue flames of his regard swept her face as he added, 'Every islander knows that it is the ghost of a ceremonial virgin who was famed as a poet and singer of supernatural talent. Men died for her hand, but her father decided that she should marry the son of the other paramount chief on Fala'isi. Unfortunately she had fallen in love with another man, a chief's son from Tonga, who had been lured here by the fame of her beauty and gifts. They ran away together, hoping to reach a sanctuary in the mountains, a temple where the goddess of love was worshipped. Her tribe found them before they got there and, in the heat of the moment, both were killed. But as they died, they sang together, a song more beautiful than anything she had composed by herself. They promised that whoever heard this song would find their true love within a year. From that moment there have always been tikau on the island. The islanders know the legend is true because the tikau is rare, it mates for life, and the birds never sing alone, but always together.'

The note of cynicism in his voice didn't quite demolish her pleasure in the innocent little myth, or the exquisite sounds of the birds' duet. However, she moved away, catching her lip in her teeth to stop it trembling. A wave of exhaustion swept over her; he noticed immediately and said brusquely, 'You look as though you've been out in the sun too long. It's not the temperate heat you're accustomed to in New Zealand, you know. Or did they not warn you about that, too?'

She said spiritedly, 'Yes, they did. There's someone every hundred yards or so on the beach giving advice and selling sunscreens.'

'Yet people still allow themselves to burn. You'd better get up to the house. Can you manage?'

'Yes! I'm just a little tired, that's all. I'm not burned, but I think I must have been out in the sun for too long. Mad dogs and New Zealanders, you know.' And she was excited, as well as scared out of her mind. Flashing a determined smile at him, she turned towards the jungle-covered bank, by now assuming cliff-like proportions in her mind. 'I'll be fine when I've had a drink and a small rest in the shade.'

One of the dogs shouldered in beside her. Insensibly comforted by its uncomplicated warmth, she put her hand on its shoulder.

He said, 'Joe,' in a voice that for all its quietness brooked no disobedience. Candace was not surprised when the animal waited until she began to follow him up the beach then settled in at her heel.

The track up the cliff was steep but well-surfaced, and she coped easily enough, although by the time they emerged on to the lawn she was exhausted, her stamina swamped in a weariness that seemed to be softening even her bones. He was right; this was no climate to deal lightly with. Will-power had no way of stopping the tiny shudders that were rippling through her.

He looked down into a face that was pale beneath the faint flush of the sun. 'Are you all right?'

'Yes, I'm fine. I don't know why I'm feeling like this.'

'I should say it's the aftermath of an adrenalin rush.' His smile was a cold, feral movement in a face carved in stark contours of strength and will-power. 'Fight or flight,' he amplified.

She bit her lip. He was right, of course; it had surged, and was now ebbing, and she couldn't afford to give in to the subsequent exhaustion.

But, excited and tired as she was, the sight of the house stopped her in her tracks. High, magnificently constructed, the thatched roof was the embodiment of authority. Great timbers supported it, leaving the wall space entirely free so that the house floated like a pavilion in a sea of lush greenery.

In the surrounding gardens the huge silken flowers of hibiscus contrasted with exotic tropical leaves and vines. One of them, the source of the sweet scent floating on the warm humid air, was the gardenia native to the island. Its small flowers glimmered amid the glossy dark leaves like earthbound stars. Banana leaves made a sharp lush punctuation in the garden, and in one corner was an enormous rain tree, its ferny leaves still open in the heat of the day, chairs and loungers scattered beneath its light shade. A great urn glazed in shades of green stood beside the fantastically coloured leaves of a plant she knew only as a small house plant. Creepers spotted with small scarlet and white flowers rioted joyously over a terrace. From somewhere came the soothing, infinitely variable sound of water, a thin musical trickle that cooled as well as pleasured the ear.

'This is lovely,' she said quietly.

'Thank you.' There was a dampening note in his voice that robbed his thanks of any warmth.

Candace felt like a snail whose horn had been flicked. All right, so he didn't think she had any right to admire his home; common politeness should, however, have persuaded him to accept her compliment with some grace. She set her mouth stubbornly. She wasn't going to allow a snub to upset her now.

However, on the threshold, she hesitated, saying when he turned an enquiring look on her, 'I'm covered in sand.'

'It won't matter, the floor's tiled.' There was more than a hint of impatience in the deep tones.

She shrugged and accompanied him in, every sense alert, eyes behind their long lashes gleaming, ears straining, skin taut, her nostrils distended as she smelt a faint hint of perfume, slightly too cloying for the tropics, and a dry, pleasant astringency that was probably the fronds used in the thatch, plus another teasingly subtle scent that was Saul Jerrard's masculine fragrance, peculiar only to him. She thought she could taste the air, warm and fresh, heavy with promise.

He walked without sound through the quiet house, much bigger inside than it seemed from the outside, spare yet opulent with dark woods and tiled floors lightened by a magnificent array of plants. The massive beams and supporting timbers were united by elaborate and beautiful sennit-work, the thatch on the outside supported by vertical lengths of bamboo. Something deep inside Candace woke to life. It was, she thought dazedly, a kind of recognition, as though all her life she had known that there was a house like this waiting for her.

Ironic that it should belong to Saul Jerrard!

Candace looked carefully about, as inconspicuously as possible searching for Stephanie, but there was no sign of her or anyone else.

She felt his eyes on her and pretended to be enthralled by a bank of plants against a wide, wooden staircase. 'It looks like a jungle,' she said softly. 'A very romantic, artfully arranged jungle.'

A sudden grin broke through the harsh mask of his features, and a potent, entirely unsuspected charm washed over her like the warm rains of the tropics, life-giving, irresistible, dangerous. Her lashes fell over eyes shadowed by confusion as she wondered at the needles of sensation arrowing uncomfortably through her body.

His smile altered in quality, something in his gaze making her profoundly edgy. But he gestured at an array of magnificent orchids. 'My housekeeper's pride and joy,' he drawled, stopping at a door. 'Would you like to wash before you have that drink?'

'Yes, I'd love to.' She cast a wry glance at her legs, the smooth golden skin filmed with a faint silver coat of salt.

'Just come back the way you came and I'll have something long and cool waiting for you.' Although there was an edged quality to his voice his smile was warm and uncomplicated, and his eyes lingered on her mouth.

She swallowed and shot into the bathroom to the sound of his soft laughter. This was one complication she hadn't even considered—but he was probably only teasing. After all, what would a man like Saul Jerrard, who was accustomed to the most beautiful women in the world, see in Candace Hume, who was attractive enough but nothing out of the ordinary? Billionaires must, she thought gloomily, have to fight women off. She ignored a tiny spoilsport voice that told her if Saul earned his living digging ditches he would still have that powerful charisma, that effortless attraction that promised so much to women.

The bathroom was small, walled and floored in pale green ceramic tiles except for one wall lined with soft, aged mirror tiles. A glance at her reflection had dismay drawing her mouth into an involuntary 'O'. She looked almost wild, her hair rioting around her small face in untamed sunshot waves, her eyes glittering, the grey irises almost swallowed by darkness. A hectic flush stained the soft red bow of her mouth and the sweep of her cheekbones, contrasting with an unusual pallor everywhere else. Her skin was oddly stretched over her neat, unimpressive features.

Somehow she looked desperate, excitement and anticipation mixing with fear and a dark foreboding. It must be this unholy cocktail that sent wires of sensation through her body, fire and ice combining to collect in her breasts and the pit of her stomach.

Clasping her hands together, she closed her eyes, willing calmness to flow out from her centre, and only when her heartbeat had slowed to regularity did she slip free from the somewhat clammy embrace of her clothes and turn on the shower.

The fittings were luxurious, but there was no opulence, no gold-plated taps or marble anywhere. Setting aside the fact that marble was far from being her favourite material, especially the highly glazed stuff that turned up nowadays in bathrooms, she decided that she felt a little cheated. There was a shower, but no shower curtain, although one wasn't needed in a room so waterproof. Plain taps, a handbasin, more orchids... Surely a man as rich as Saul Jerrard should indulge in a little sybaritic ostentation?

The tempting little smile that had curved her lips faded as she visualised him. No, for all his filthy lucre he had an air of inborn, totally understated authority that was primitive in its impact. No doubt it came in very useful in the cut-throat world of high finance. But her uncontrollable imagination pictured him in less sophisticated surroundings, splendidly naked in some dense jungle, stronger light from a younger sun sliding in rich colour over the leanly muscled build only hinted at by his clothes...

A spasm of awareness speared through her body. Without volition her eyes flew to her mirrored reflection; horrified, she watched a flush of excitement rise from her peaking breasts to her throat.

'No,' she whispered, all erotic imagery banished in an instant by sheer panic. She could not afford this. Oh, she knew what it was. Magazines were so frank now that none of the signs of sexual arousal were unknown to her even though she had never experienced them before. She had, she thought in hurried torment, made sure of that.

Rejected with decisive finality by those she had loved in her childhood, she had never made a conscious decision to avoid the ultimate intimacy with any man, she had just subconsciously made sure she was never in a situation where her hidden desires could be activated. One of her friends once told her that she reminded her of Kipling's cat, who walked by its wild lone. Candace had laughed and protested, but since then she had noticed that she always set a limit to emotional and physical intimacy, beyond which she allowed no one, male or female. From the age of ten she had watched the world from behind barricades, determined never to allow anyone inside, concede to any person the power to hurt her again.

And it had worked. She enjoyed her life. She liked working in the library of a big industrial firm. And for the last three years she had had a purpose, a quest to fulfil. Which, she told herself as she settled down to scrubbing, was one of the reasons why this inconvenient response to Saul Jerrard was going to have to be overcome.

A tap on the door made her cower behind the curtain of water, but it was a feminine voice, albeit a deep one, that called her name. Her heart went into overdrive. Stephanie? 'Yes, who is it?' she squeaked, peering through the spray of water.

'Ailu.' The door opened and a large, unsmiling Polynesian woman came in carrying a length of pale green cotton, batik-printed in shades of copper and rose.

Shattering disappointment must have shown for a moment in Candace's expression, but she managed to overcome it enough to say, with incongruous politeness, 'How do you do? I'm Candace Hume.'

Still no smile. The woman said evenly, 'I know. Mr Saul suggested you might like to have your clothes washed, so I've brought you this sarong to wear until they're dry.'

'That's kind of him. And you. Thank you.' It was difficult to retain any dignity when she was stark naked behind a transparent curtain of water, but she essayed another smile, which was rebuffed with the same monumental aloofness.

Abashed, and a little angry, she stayed silent while her clothes were picked up and Ailu went out. Then the fear came gibbering back. Perhaps they knew...

No, they could not. There was no way they could find out who she was and what she wanted. And she couldn't lose her nerve now. These next few minutes were vital; she had to convince Saul Jerrard that she was harmless and a fit person for his young sister to associate with, and she had to make some sort of pleasant impression on Stephanie.

Folding her lips into a determined line, she dried herself down and wound the cotton around her body. Two days on Fala'isi had convinced her that the sarong was a useful method of covering nakedness and keeping cool, and she had bought several, though none in so fine material as this. With the purchases had come instructions for making sure they stayed decent. She gathered the free end carefully, wriggled out the other from beneath the tight border, and tied them together in a knot between her breasts so that it looked like a strapless sunfrock, the supple material gracefully indicating her narrow waist and the sleek line of her hips and thighs.

Perfectly decent, she assured her reflection. She didn't need a bra, and, although she would have felt much more comfortable wearing a pair of pants, the housekeeper had taken hers off to wash, and really, the material was not transparent—no one could see that she was quite naked under it.

She drew a deep breath. Nothing ventured, nothing gained. But oh, such a lot depended on how she behaved now.

He was coming along the passage when she walked through the door, a dark figure every bit as forbidding as the fearsome ancestor mask that loomed over him. Her palms wet, she set off self-consciously towards him, her skin prickling at the searching assessment he made no attempt to hide. Nerves gave a fugitive colour to her skin, sent a tingle down her spinal cord as she met those incredible eyes with all of the composure she could muster.

I don't like you, she thought suddenly, defiantly.

Her chin lifted. With a backbone as straight as a wand she gave him a direct look, uncaring for a moment of the great stakes she was playing for.

He stopped as she came up, his expression calm and remote, then smiled; the irresistible charm washed over her in an invigorating flood that put bubbles in her blood and set off chimes of small bells in her heart.

'You look like an islander,' he said, lifting a hand to touch for a moment the gold-streaked curl at her temple. 'Smaller, much more slender, but with the same straight back and smooth, swaying walk. Still thirsty?'

'I think I could drink a tank dry.' Her voice was slightly husky. Feeling an absolute fool, she swallowed to try to clear it.

'Oh, I can offer you something much more appetising than a tank.'

She hesitated, then said with a shy upward glance through her lashes, 'You're being very kind. Thank you.'

His hand moved to her elbow as he strode with those silent panther steps beside her. 'Castaways are always taken care of in the South Seas. It's a local tradition.'

She reacted to the dry note in the deep voice with another doubtful look, but although he was smiling his eyes were so dazzling that no emotion was discernible. Somewhere deep inside her a tiny trigger set off an alarm. His fingers at her elbow felt like fetters instead of the loose, impersonal grip of courtesy.

'After all,' he said musingly, 'my distant ancestor was almost a castaway. He arrived here during a hurricane in a ship that was as near a wreck as made no difference. And he was welcomed and made much of. Of course, he had to marry the last paramount chief's daughter...'

# CHAPTER THREE

CANDACE'S eyes wide with interest, she said, 'Did he really?'

A sardonic smile quirked at the corner of Saul's mouth. 'Yes. Family history has it that neither was particularly thrilled at the match, but the decision was not theirs to make. Anyway, also according to family tradition, the marriage, although volatile, was a very happy one.'

'That would be the Chapman ancestor,' she said, nodding.

'Yes. You've heard of him?'

She hesitated a fraction of a second but managed to recover. 'Everyone who arrives on Fala'isi knows that the Chapmans have been here forever, and I heard somewhere that you were related to them.'

'Grant is my cousin,' he said without expression.

The fingers at her elbow tightened as he steered her through a wide door on to a terrace shaded by yet another bank of orchids, exquisitely beautiful flowers, all white, like moon butterflies poised gracefully on long stems. It didn't, Candace thought with a sudden rush of poignancy, seem fair that one man should be able to surround himself with such loveliness when there were people who lived in abject squalor and misery.

Making an odd little grimace, she looked away, swallowing as her eyes found the pitcher, glowing golden with tiny runlets of moisture frosting its straight sides. 'Oh, that looks blissful,' she sighed.

'Do you want it straight, or with something to ginger it up?'

She smiled. 'Straight, please. I have no head for alcohol, and if I'm going to get that cat back to the beach before they send out a search party, I'll——'

'Oh, don't worry about that, it's been organised. I'll take you back, and the yacht will be on the beach in time for the first tourist tomorrow morning.'

She blushed deeply, mortified more by a guilty conscience than the faint note of condemnation in his even tone. 'That's very kind of you, but I can't——'

'Of course you can,' he said, smiling down at her with amused arrogance. 'It's too late, anyway. Everything's arranged. I promise you I'll behave with as much propriety as you want, but of course you'll have dinner with me.'

How to deal with this? Of course, she wanted to have dinner there, but he had said 'me', not 'us'. Where were the others, the snobbish Lydia, and Stephanie? Biting back the question that hovered on the tip of her tongue, she said, 'That's very kind of you but I don't want to be a nuisance.' Flustered by the faint lift of his eyebrows, she continued, 'I mean, I know you're not alone, and I don't—I can't——'

'Oh, don't worry about the others,' he said casually. 'Lydia flew back to England yesterday, and my sister is not here tonight.'

Fighting desperately to prevent the shattering disappointment from showing in her expression, she drank some of the tropical fruit juice he had poured for her. The cool, not too sweet liquid slid soothingly down her dry throat. She drained the glass, using the time to gather her confidence about her, so that when she set it down she was able to smile at him and say with sunny insouciance, 'I really couldn't put you to such bother, Mr Jerrard. You've been very kind, but I don't want to intrude on your privacy.'

'Nonsense,' he said, his eyes gleaming as they rested on her curving mouth. 'You'll save me from a dull evening spent by myself, and if you object to being treated as a diversion, well, perhaps you owe it to me. For being so kind?'

She didn't want to stay. Every instinct warned her that he had some hidden agenda. Was he bored now that the glamorous Lydia was no longer in tow? Uncomfortably she looked past him to the smooth sweep of grass, edged by luxuriant plants in a serene, dense border.

It was highly unlikely that he was attracted to her; she knew she was not beautiful, and she wasn't the sort of sophisticated woman he apparently liked, if Lydia Woolcott was any example—well-skilled in the arts of dalliance. She had never even made love!

A strange hot thrill numbed her mind. She sent him an uncertain glance and saw that he was smiling slightly, his beautiful mouth curved in recognition, it seemed, of her dilemma.

Some time ago she had read an article about the world Saul Jerrard inhabited. It had shocked and dismayed her, with its flippant dismissal of marriage as a business contract and love saved for romances outside the marriage bed. She remembered thinking disdainfully that if that was sophistication she wanted none of it.

But if she turned tail and fled, she might lose any chance of furthering her acquaintance with Jerrard. After all, she thought robustly, even if he did hope for some sort of romantic interlude, he would accept her polite refusal. Some primeval instinct told her that he wasn't the sort to use force with a woman. And if her instinct was wrong, if he tried anything, she knew a few tricks that would make him change his mind.

Making up her mind with a snatch of recklessness, she grinned pertly up at him, and said, 'In that case, I can hardly say no, can I? Thank you, I'd love to have dinner with you.'

He was perfectly still for a second, before giving her another slow smile that set those damned alarm bells

jangling again. Unless Saul Jerrard was a natural phil-
anderer, born with the compulsive need to flirt, something she didn't really believe, he was definitely trying
to charm her.

It was difficult to stay aloof, as she had fully intended, and even more difficult to keep him at a safe
distance. To begin with, he was an interesting conver-
sationalist. As they sat watching the sun sink behind the
graceful tangle of coconut palms he told her a little more
of that first Chapman, part pirate, part explorer, part
man of conscience, who had arrived here when the
islanders were reeling from their first taste of European
civilisation, with its attendant scourges of plague and
greed.

'There were very few of them left by the time he got
here,' he said, topping up her glass. 'Many had been
forced by various villains to dive for black pearls in the
lagoon until they developed the bends and died. More
were killed by measles, or mumps, or influenza, illnesses
to which they had no resistance. The epidemics wiped
out almost all of the chiefly class, and weakened those
who were left. The whole social system of the island was
in ruins when Chapman arrived. The few people who
were left were desperate for someone to help them
organise against the assorted riff-raff and scum who were
preying on them. He found a pitiful remnant hiding in
the hills, demoralised, ill, their only hope a legend that
in their hour of greatest need a man would come from
their enemies and marry a virgin of the line of the paramount chiefs, and he would save them.'

She made a fascinated little noise. 'Was that some
relative of the poet and singer? The woman who died
and became the tikau?'

He lounged back into his chair, watching her indol-
ently, one hand stretched out along the armrest. Light
danced through the heavy canopy of the vine above them,
summoning flakes of colour in his hair, dark fire to go

with the blue fire of his eyes, creating shadows across the fleshless contours of his face, emphasising the darkly dangerous magnetism.

'A direct descendant.'

'But you said they died,' she objected.

'Apparently not without consummating their love, and bearing a daughter,' he drawled, his eyes half closed. 'She was the ancestress of the paramount line. And yes, this virgin was a direct descendant of their daughter.'

'Do you believe that?'

He said smoothly, 'You must agree it's a very convenient legend. It links the ruling line to an ancestor who had immense mana, as well as one of the chiefly families of Tonga.'

'But you don't believe it?'

'As it happens, I do. I must admit to a few reservations about the transformation of the lovers to a pair of birds, though.'

Her delighted chuckle was a rich sound on the somnolent air. 'I think perhaps I do, too,' she confessed. 'Why did the first Chapman come to Fala'isi?'

'Alas, apparently for exactly the same reason as all the other flotsam. He wanted black pearls, sandalwood and trepang for the Chinese trade, but he was a curious man, imbued with the desire to explore, and made the mistake of going into the hinterland. While he was there he came upon a pool, and he saw the last ceremonial virgin, whose name was Sula, bathing in it. There are two versions of what happened next. One says that he was so smitten he followed her to her refuge in the high mountains and asked for her hand in marriage, was recognised as the hero of the legend, and persuaded by his wife to stay and protect them.'

She had been listening with a fascinated interest, but something in his tone made her guess, 'But you don't believe that.'

He sent her a lazy, sardonic look. 'The other version says that he raped her by the pool, and was taken prisoner and forced into marriage at the point of a spear.'

'I don't like that version.'

'Women don't,' he said idly. 'However, I must admit it seems more likely to me. He was no hero, but a man who had survived—and prospered—in the hell-hole that was the Pacific of his day, which indicated a considerable ruthlessness. I've no doubt he assumed she was an ordinary Polynesian woman with their open enjoyment of the delights of the flesh. Anyway, whatever happened, he found himself married to her, and regarded by her people as their saviour.'

'So that's what he became.' She was intrigued by this very human hero.

He grinned. 'Yes, apparently a reluctant saviour. His marriage gave him the mana or prestige to organise a sort of militia from the few fighting men left. It also gave his children chiefly mana, which is why my cousin is the paramount chief of the island today. Our ancestor's own mana he acquired himself through his efforts to make Fala'isi safe.'

'He sounds—fascinating.' Candace was unable to prevent herself from visualising Saul as that piratical ancestor. He had the looks, and the aura of strength and ruthlessness, as well as the pragmatic intelligence.

'His methods wouldn't bear much scrutiny, not even in those days,' Saul told her somewhat grimly. 'He was neither a romantic figure, nor a virtuous one, but in the South Pacific a hundred and fifty years ago scruples were a distinct disadvantage. Within a very short time everyone, pearlers, trepang fishermen, sandalwood thieves, knew it was not worth looking for trouble—or anything else—at Fala'isi, unless they were prepared to pay fair rates for it. He organised the pearl trade so effectively that it's still run on the system he set up.'

Something in his voice, some hidden note of envy, resonated through her. Without thinking she guessed, 'You would have liked to be that first Chapman, wouldn't you?'

His beautifully moulded mouth twisted into an indulgent smile. 'Why, because of the derring-do? My life has enough drama in it to keep me busy. It's not so colourful, in that I don't wade around in buckets of blood and the knives aimed at my back aren't made of steel, but the wars are just as deadly, and the responsibility every bit as acute. As is the necessity to protect those who depend on me.'

So the man was a romantic. Candace was stunned.

He caught the look of shock on her face and enquired drily, 'Does that surprise you? Perhaps you thought that those of us who have corporate responsibilities wear horns and stamp across the world with hobnailed boots?'

Spiritedly she retorted, 'I've never really given it any thought, except when I read another horror story about someone with more money than sense cutting down another million acres of tropical jungle, or outbidding others just as rich and pretentious to buy a tasteless chunk of rock too big to wear.'

'So you've never wondered bitterly why some people own more than their share of the world's goods?'

She wouldn't back down, although there was a very definite taunt in the deep flexible voice. 'Anyone who's wondered where they're going to get the money for a new dress has asked themselves that, just as any sane person has wondered why they should have the luck to be born whole and healthy and in a country where the desert is not trying to swallow up all the arable land. In a perfect world there would be no poor and no plutocrats, but the world is not perfect. And I'm not stupid or rigid enough to think I have any answers, let alone all of them. Provided laws and public opinion are able to prevent the worst excesses of the rich and the powerful, the wasteful squandering of resources and the cruel use of power, then people like you can't cause too much harm.'

Against the glare of the evening sky his eyes were narrowed, mere slivers of incandescent blue fire behind his lashes, yet she felt the saliva dry in her mouth.

Huskily, she said, 'I didn't mean that exactly the way it sounded.'

'Oh, don't spoil it by backing down,' he said lightly. 'And I agree. In a perfect world there would be no hunger, no pain and sorrow, but until that day comes I'll protect the responsibilities entrusted to me with every resource at my disposal.'

'Just for a company?' she marvelled, impelled for some stupid reason to push him.

'Do you know how many people depend on Jerrard's?' His voice bit into her composure, each one cool and contemptuous. 'There are governments that rely on us to keep them stable. We have been able to push for human rights, insist on unpopular conservation measures, persuade governments to force through laws to prevent the degradation of women and children because we are an enormously rich, powerful organisation, with money and goods and services that governments need.'

Candace swallowed, easing the harshness in her throat. She said quietly, 'Obviously I was out of line.'

'No.' His voice was tired and flat. 'Merely following the usual line. We have made mistakes, but rarely the same one twice, and in spite of all the propaganda we try to make decisions that take the welfare of all people into account.'

'I see.'

He shrugged. 'I should be used to flak by now, I deal with it every day, and now Stephanie is at the age where she is worried about owning, as she puts it, an indecent amount of the world's money.'

'The idealistic teens,' she said softly, a little smile tugging at the corner of her mouth. 'I remember. You think you can change the world. One of the first great moments of disillusion is when you realise you can't.' And because it hurt in some obscure way that he should be affected by Stephanie's attitude, she said lightly, 'And even if you don't, I must confess that I envy your ancestor. In spite of everything, I think it was a simpler world then. I'd love to be my own mistress, swashbuckling across an unknown, undiscovered world, captain of my own fate.'

'It sounds like every man's secret fantasy. I thought women preferred security,' he returned drily.

'I don't believe in security. A tidal wave could come up over the edge of the ocean five minutes from now and drown us both. Security comes from within, it has nothing to do with the outside world.'

She spoke passionately, her voice coloured by memories, and realised with shock that he was watching her closely from behind the thick fringe of his lashes, his shaman's eyes narrowed shards of sapphire.

'A hard lesson to learn,' he said, breaking a silence that had stretched too long.

Uncomfortably she shrugged. 'But a necessary one. The world is not hostile, it's just indifferent. And we are as much bound by its laws as the pearl oysters at the bottom of the lagoon.'

'So eat, drink, and be merry, because tomorrow we die?'

A tiny shudder worked its way up her spine. Her shoulders lifted in another small shrug as she countered with what she hoped was an ironic smile, 'No, not exactly. That's asking for trouble—what if tomorrow we don't die?'

He smiled, his teeth very white in the austere planes and angles of his face. 'A pragmatic romantic! An interesting combination. Tell me, what do you do back in Auckland?'

'I'm a library clerk,' she said politely.

'Public?'

She shook her head. 'No, I work for a big mining and industrial concern.'

'I might know them. Who are they?'

For some reason she hesitated, but there was really no reason why he shouldn't know. 'March and Osborne. They have fingers in all sorts of pies, gold-mining, oil prospecting, a steel mill—almost anything to do with minerals.'

'And do you find it interesting?'

'Yes, but if I want to go any further I'll have to finish my degree.'

'Finish?'

She did not normally discuss her life with strangers, but she explained, 'I did two years of a history degree, but then I got—oh, restless, I suppose. I dropped out and went across to England, spent a year travelling around.'

Her adoptive mother, impelled by who knew what guilt, had tracked her down, and forced enough money on her to pay for a round-the-world airline ticket. At first, rigid with a sense of betrayal, Candace had thrown the money back in her face, but her mother had wept, and soft-heartedly Candace had accepted.

Seeing again the woman she had called mother for the first ten years of her life had opened a door on to her past that had refused to close. Angry and restless, she had been unable to settle at university, finally leaving for overseas.

With an ever-changing group of acquaintances she had made her way from youth hostel to youth hostel around the great cities of Europe, revelling in the history and culture, the beauty and the awe-inspiring age.

It was while there that she had realised how lacking in background she was. When she arrived back she had set out to discover her birth parents.

It had been a long and tortuous path, leading to a grave in a tiny village in Poverty Bay where her mother lay with the husband she had married a year after Candace was born. They had been married for less than ten years when they died, her mother committing suicide shortly after her husband had drowned on a fishing expedition.

Candace had wept for them both, but especially for her mother, who had been forced to adopt out her first, illegitimate child, only to take her own life so soon after she had attained 'respectability'.

From thence Candace had searched for her father, only to discover that he had been an orphan who'd fled to Australia six months before her birth. And there the trail had run cold. But ultimately, it was her quest that had brought her to Fala'isi, and to a man who was watching her with that narrowed intent stare, as though she were a creature from some other planet.

As no doubt she was to him, she thought flippantly.

'And what will you do if you finish your history degree?'

She shook her head. Then, without even thinking, she said, 'I'll grow flowers.'

His head inclined slightly. 'Just like that?'

Startled herself, she murmured, 'I love flowers and gardens, and I like growing things. Yes, that's what I'll do. I'll find a job in a nursery and when I'm ready I'll set up for myself.'

'How?'

Embarrassed, she answered lightly, 'Oh, there's always a way. There are ways of achieving anything; all one has to do is discover them.'

A *frisson* tightened her skin. She didn't have to look at him to know that he was watching her. Made profoundly uncomfortable, she pulled the thin cotton a little further over her knees. She could feel that survey, knew exactly when it lingered on the smooth length of legs defined too well by the sarong, then swung to her breasts and the sleek lines of her throat and cheek. Bubbles of nervous exhilaration squeezed through her veins.

Determined not to give in to his silent intimidation, she looked firmly out to sea. By now the sun was well down, and the evening hush had set in; no birds called from the clear sky or the shadowed jungle. The only sound was the muted boom of the Pacific rollers as they dashed themselves to death on the barrier reef.

She had been conscious that all through the conversation, like the mysterious undercurrents in an apparently smooth river, had run another form of communication, as though their bodies were conducting a different, hidden dialogue. Bewildered and alarmed, for this was something she had never encountered before, she tried to detach herself from it, ignoring the bone-deep responses to unknown stimuli that were sending sharp thrills of sensation through her body.

It had been possible to ignore it while they were talking, but now, when the silence of dusk pressed down on them, she had to face the fact that she was strangely, potently affected by him.

Unable to keep her eyes away, she allowed them to drift, oh, so casually, so slowly, back to him. He was smiling a wolf's smile, the hard masculine angles of his face unsoftened. It took all of her will-power to meet that laser probe steadily. Dazzled, wary, she was determined not to let him see how hard it was to hold her lashes steady, keep the small smile pinned firmly to lips that wanted only to tremble.

Something powerful, not to be denied, moved in the pit of her stomach. The attraction she had been fighting from the moment she had seen him in the restaurant took a quantum leap into desire.

The ready colour fled from her skin. Desire was the wild card, the devil in the pack. Her birth mother had desired too much, and she had been the result. It was desire, ferocious, uncontrollable, that had led her adoptive parents to abandon her. From the time she was old enough to understand what havoc it could wreak, she had determined never to become a slave to it. It hadn't been too difficult; she had merely kept well away from any man who might have set up that forbidden pulse of attraction.

Which made it doubly ironic that it should be Stephanie's brother who had infiltrated her defences— or perhaps, she thought, desperately trying to infuse some sort of logic into her emotions, it was because he was Stephanie's brother. He had slipped under her guard. She had set her sights so definitely on Stephanie that she hadn't really noticed his impact on her until it was too late.

Her eyes returned to the western sky where the sun was giving up its battle with the darkness in a torrid extravaganza of scarlet and gold, fiercely pure colours that laid a gloss of magic over the scene.

'It's so beautiful,' she said softly.

'Where "every prospect pleases, And only man is vile,"' he quoted mockingly as he got up. 'Come on out to the edge of the cliff. You'll get a much better view from there.'

Telling herself firmly that in a few hours she would be back at the hotel and she would not see him again, she accompanied him across the lawn, stopping beneath the spreading branches of a kapok tree.

The sunset was glorious, the warm air wafting the scent of the sea mingled with the lush fecundity of the forest below, the light from the sun sliding over them in slabs of coral and gold, gilding their features so that they looked for a few fantastic seconds like statues from some decadent ancient civilisation.

Then it was over, the darkness fell in a cloak of humid air, and he said, 'We'd better go back inside before Ailu wonders what's happened to us.'

One of the dogs came bounding up. Candace went to put out her hand but he said sharply, 'No. They're guard dogs, not pets. All right, Joe.'

Her hand fell to her side; she watched as the dog disappeared into the darkness.

For all Saul's power and the wonderful things he could buy with his money, he was as much a prisoner as any man without the money to live fully and happily. His prison might be luxurious and beautiful, filled with toys, but it was still a prison.

He must have seen her shiver, for he said coolly, 'There are always people who want to profit from the rich.'

'Or the powerful,' she said quietly, conscious of his glance on her.

'Is it the power you disapprove of?'

'I—yes, I suppose it is.'

'But there are so many different forms of power,' he pointed out. 'Look at the power being a parent gives. Or a lover.'

'Yes, but that power is restricted. A parent doesn't have many children, and a lover is freely, willingly, granted his or her power. You, by an accident of birth——'

'And a lot of hard work.'

'All right, then, a lot of hard work as well, control an enormous amount of power. I'm not saying you misuse it, but you must admit that other people in your position have.'

'I do admit it, although I think you'd probably find that more human misery has been caused by politicians than by businessmen. However, most institutions and systems have checks and balances to prevent the continual misuse of power. That applies to me, too.'

Recklessly, she persisted, 'But you could get away with almost anything. What is there to stop you?'

'That system I spoke of,' he said drily. 'Shall we take a hypothetical incident? Let's say that I kidnap you and take you off to a love-nest up in the mountains and there have my evil way with you. Do you honestly think I could get away with it?'

Candace felt as though she had walked into a trap. His voice had dropped to a deep sensuous purr, but there was an undertone of some concentrated emotion that set the hairs on the back of her neck rising.

'Well, I doubt if anyone at the hotel would object,' she said, trying hard to make her tone light, almost amused. 'Even if they did wonder, you have your cousin with his special kind of power on this island to protect you.'

'And when I finally released you, having sated myself in the silken delights of your beautiful body? No doubt you would run straight to the police?'

'I would indeed,' she said stoutly, firmly repressing the delicious shiver of anticipation his words—no, more his tone, the barely concealed rasp in his voice, was causing deep in the fork of her body.

They had reached a darkened terrace outside one of the rooms; he stopped and turned to her, an outline in the sudden tropical darkness, a primitive threat that set her nerves jangling again.

She hurried into speech. 'But somehow I think it would be difficult to convince the local police that you had— that it was——'

'Rape?' He pronounced the word with a certain distaste. 'I think perhaps you underestimate their devotion to justice. If they didn't seem inclined to bring me to justice, what would you do then?'

She bit her lip, sensing those undercurrents again, dark and murky and alarming. 'I don't know—what would there be to do? Go home, I suppose.' Her voice firmed.

'Women have always had great difficulty convincing others that they have been raped.'

'True, but try to repress your feminism for a second. Why not go to the newspapers?'

She blinked, searching his face in the darkness, wondering at this odd conversation. After a moment she said huskily, 'No, I——'

'Why?'

The word cracked out like a whip. It was like being cross-examined. Her chin lifted as in a voice only one degree above frigid she said, 'Would any newspaper dare to lose your favour?'

He laughed. 'Ever heard of the freedom of the Press? Yes, there are certainly newspapers that would publish a juicy little bit of gossip like that.'

She recalled headlines she had seen in some of the gutter Press and shuddered. 'No. It would make me feel—unclean. And, if you don't mind, I don't like this conversation. I'm willing to agree that I could at the very least make you feel uncomfortable.'

At first she thought he was going to continue, but after a tense moment he said merely, 'There are always avenues for revenge, Candace.'

Strangely enough, that sounded like a threat too. Alarmed all over again she went with him into the room behind the terrace, looking around her with elaborate interest as the lights flowered. The room was huge, five of the six sides being open to the night. There were no windows, their place being taken by immense widths of finely slatted blinds, rolled up still to give the air free play. No mats covered the ochre-brown tiles, and the furniture was modern, wood-framed chairs and sofas covered with white calico.

Everywhere plants in an impressive array of pots lent their welcome greenery to the room. An urn glazed by some mysterious process with starbursts of deep glowing indigo on a slate-blue ground picked up and emphasised the blues in a painting by Gauguin; the calm Polynesian faces of the women in it were impassive yet sensual as they gazed across the gulf of time and culture to the present.

There were sculptures, some starkly modern, one magnificent reclining woman in wood as black as ebony, and above it all soared the spectacular roof, as decorative as anything else in the room.

Candace's tense body pulsed with restless urgency, her whole being longing for some unknown experience, the blood coursing too fast through her veins. A vagrant breeze whispered into the room, bearing with it the dim sound of distant drums and the plaintive notes of a birdcall, like the dying sob of a violin. Not a tikau bird, but it pulled at her heart-strings.

This, she told herself sternly, is why those old sea captains had such a terrible time keeping their crews once they reached the South Seas. This is the lure of the South Pacific, age-old, narcotic, and bloody dangerous, and you're no more immune to it than they were!

And that had to be it. The attraction she felt was nothing more than the usual interest felt by receptive woman for virile man, intensified by the romantic situation. When it was looked at in that way, she had really been getting herself in a great tizz over nothing.

'That,' he murmured, 'is an odd look.'

She smiled, confidence returning in a great rush. 'Really? I didn't see it, so I don't know. This is a lovely room.'

His mouth curled, but he followed her cue smoothly, and until after the delicious dinner served beneath the stars on a long porch he treated her with the polite impersonality of a host for a guest. Her self-possession came back; really, she had been stupid, worrying about the effect he had on her nerves. Attraction was a physical thing, born in the genes, as instinctive as the desire to eat. For the first time in her life she had been confronted with a dynamically potent man, and at a time when she was rendered vulnerable by her meeting with Stephanie. Naturally she had over-reacted.

Relief made her sparkle; she ate heartily of the exquisite meal served to her, drank a little very good white wine, and found that it was easy enough to respond to his urbane worldliness. She even found herself teasing him, her small face irradiated with laughter. He wasn't used to it, she could tell, but his wizard's eyes gleamed with amusement as he responded.

However, when he poured her more wine she shook her head, holding her hands to her flushed cheeks for a regretful moment. 'No, it's delicious, but I've had more than enough. Whenever I feel as though I'm in a permanent blush I know I've reached my limit.'

'Wise girl.'

She lifted haughty brows. 'Woman, thank you.'

'Sorry. But like that, with your face flushed and your eyes sleepy, you look about fifteen.'

She gave a weary sigh. 'I know. It's the bane of my life! But I'm twenty-three. How old are you?'

'Thirty-three.'

'It's unusual, surely, for a man of your age to end up heading an organisation as big and influential as Jerrard's?'

The broad shoulders moved in a slight shrug, but his eyes never left hers. 'It's what I was trained to do, although I never thought I'd have to take over so soon. After my parents died the board wanted to chop up the organisation into its constituents, dismembering the entity my father had worked so hard to build. I couldn't allow that, and fortunately I had the power to swing the balance, but it's been a hard slog.'

Had it hardened him, or had he been born hard? Her eyes drifted slowly over his face, searching out the features that made such an instant impression on everyone who saw him. Had those striking, hawklike features ever been softened in a baby face? It was hard to imagine him as a child. Had Saul ever looked tenderly at anyone other than his sister?

# CHAPTER FOUR

'HARD slog sounds like a typical English under-statement,' Candace said, raising her brows. 'I seem to remember reading something about it in the newspapers. According to them it was more like war to the death.'

Saul smiled, bringing her skin out in goose-pimples. It was a repeat of that humourless wolf's smile. 'Oh, I like a challenge,' he said softly.

Heartfelt fervour coloured her voice. 'I don't. Not like that, anyway. I'm all for a nice placid life.'

He grinned. It was not a nice grin, but there was a flash of humour in it when he said, 'Rubbish. You've got that look, however hard you try to hide it beneath those demure lashes.'

'That look?' Honestly bewildered, she made the mistake of looking directly at him, but her puzzled eyes met only limpid amusement.

'That reckless look,' he said softly. 'All the best pirates had it. And more than that, you have a distinctly wilful mouth. I find it almost impossible to believe that you want a placid life.'

'Next,' she scoffed, unaccountably stimulated by his words and the way his eyes lingered on her mouth as he said them, 'you'll be telling me you believe in phrenology!'

'Because I say you have an audacious air? Didn't phrenologists judge people by the bumps on their heads?'

'The same principle as judging them by their mouths,' she returned tartly.

'So you don't like being told you're impetuous? I wonder why. A few minutes ago you were telling me you'd like to be my extremely reckless ancestor, sailing the seas of an unknown world.'

She shot him a nervous look. He was still smiling, this time with enjoyment at having backed her into a corner of her own making. 'Oh, well,' she said offhandedly, 'I suppose you might be right, although somehow my romantic desire for freedom seems to fade a little when it's transferred to the twentieth century!'

His quiet laughter was interrupted by Ailu, who appeared at the door with a tray. She floated majestically in, set the tray on a glass table before Candace, and said, 'Your clothes are ready now, madam. I've put them in the bathroom.'

'Thank you.' Candace essayed another smile, was met with the same cool courtesy that had chilled her to the bones before, and as she watched the woman disappear through the door said thoughtfully, 'I wonder why she doesn't like me.'

'Do you need to be liked by everyone?'

She shrugged. 'I don't enjoy such obvious disapproval.'

'Ailu has had to deal with women who would do almost anything to get in here. You must excuse her if she's suspicious at first. Would you like to pour?'

It sounded more like a direct order than a request. The coffee-pot was heavy and she hid her flushed cheeks by bending over the cups as she poured, because of course the housekeeper had every reason to be suspicious. Oh, she had no designs on Saul, but she definitely had an ulterior reason for storming the barricades of his privacy.

He took his coffee with milk but no sugar, fairly strong. When they had drunk it she said with determination, 'I must get back to the hotel now. Could I ring a taxi?'

'No, my driver will take you back.'

'No, no.' She was embarrassed. 'Honestly, I got myself here, I'll get back.'

'But you stayed here because I asked you to,' he pointed out, smiling a little mockingly. 'Don't worry, it's only a few miles for Gil to go.'

With reluctance she yielded the issue, walking out with him into the darkness when the car drew up outside. The moon was high in the blue-black sky, embedded in the Milky Way like a great pearl on a diamond band. Out on the lagoon lightfishers went about their work, weaving patterns like fireflies across the water. The thin line of the reef was startlingly white against the darkness of the ocean. It was overwhelming, so beautiful that it caught her throat.

Impulsively, she said, 'I've had a lovely day. Thank you for being so kind.'

'My pleasure.' He even sounded as though he meant it.

The driver was silent all the way to the motel, and when he opened the door to let her out he responded to her tentative smile with the same aloof courtesy as the housekeeper. But then, security men of all kinds were trained to be distrustful, she reassured herself as she went in and collected her key.

'Had a good day?' the receptionist asked chattily.

'Lovely, thank you.'

'Nice place, Mr Jerrard's, so I've heard.'

Candace looked at her, met a cheerful but knowing smile, and cursed the colour that heated her cheeks. 'Yes, lovely,' she said distantly, and walked away.

How had the woman known where she spent the afternoon?

Oh, you're being paranoid, she told herself severely. Fala'isi is probably like any small town, everyone knows everyone else. The man who rents out the boats is probably her husband. Or her cousin, or the boy who first kissed her...

But once in her room she went into the minuscule bathroom and splashed cold water on her hot cheeks before looking at her watch. It was still quite early, only nine o'clock, and she felt far too keyed up to go to bed yet.

'Washing,' she said out loud, her eyes falling on the neat bag that held her used clothes. She stood quite still, staring at it with unfocused eyes, her brain working furiously. Something niggled at her, some vague and inchoate unease that refused to be categorised. After a moment she shrugged. Rampant paranoia, she scoffed as she went off down to the laundry-room. Saul Jerrard was quite enough to make any woman uneasy, and excited, and profoundly wary. Rich food, she thought, and I don't mean the dinner.

Almost an hour later she was back in her room putting her clean clothes away. When it was done she looked a little desperately around the small, neat, impersonal area. Restlessness ached in her bones, tugging at her nerves, jagging through her body. With an impatient angry gesture she switched off the light and went over to the window, pulling the curtain back to stand there.

Fala'isi was not the sort of place where you could find things to do all twenty-four hours of the day, but even so it was far from asleep yet. Sounds of mirth came from the pool, a few high-pitched shrieks, and the laughter that inevitably followed. Not too far away music throbbed, the melody lost on the heavy air, only the insistent beating of the drums travelling as far as the motel. Then a group of islanders sang as they walked past the motel, their magnificent harmonies blending to drown out the disco beat.

She sighed, her eyes filling with stupid tears, and turned away, letting the curtain fall behind her.

Sleep came easily enough, yet she woke in the morning with that pinprick of apprehension magnified. In the dim light of early dawn she tried to track it down. It was nothing to do with Saul, nothing to do with the Jerrards at all. It had made itself obvious when she came up to her room. Her brows pleated as she retraced her steps of the night before, into the bathroom, picking up the clothes bag—that was it! Yesterday morning when she had organised her clothes for laundering she had put a pair of tennis socks beside the bag so that she would remember to handwash them.

And last night they had been halfway down the bag.

Someone had been poking around her clothes. Her stomach curled. Who on earth——?

Galvanised, she sprang out of bed and searched through her room, shaking out her clothes, checking to make sure that everything was in its correct place. Nothing had been disturbed, not a thing was out of place, and she sank back on to her bed, frowning even as she enjoyed the relief that washed over her. Not that she owned anything of value to a thief; her clothes were mostly standard summer cottons, and even the dress she had worn to the restaurant was nothing a thief would want to steal. She had some pretty costume jewellery, but it was worth very little, and all of her valuables, her passport and tickets and travellers' cheques were stored in the hotel safe.

It had probably been the maid. Yes, that was what must have happened. The woman had knocked the bag over when she was cleaning and, not realising the socks had been left outside, and piled them in with the other clothes.

But she went down to check that everything was still there in the safe. And of course it was. Feeling foolish, she smiled at the receptionist, who looked a little surprised when she made no attempt to take any of the cheques with her. The woman smiled back, then a subtle change in her eyes and expression warned Candace of someone behind her. The smile widened, became complicated, and the dark eyes dilated.

Candace moved aside, starting a little when Saul said smoothly, 'Ah, Candace, you're back.'

Her heart lurched. 'I—ah, I haven't been anywhere,' she said foolishly.

His lazy smile was belied by his intent look. 'I tried to contact you last night but there was no answer.'

'Oh. I was down in the laundry.'

'That explains it,' he said gravely, although there was laughter in his eyes. 'Am I stopping you from conducting some business?'

She looked at the receptionist, who was unashamedly listening. 'I—no,' she said. 'I've finished, thank you.'

The receptionist flashed a smile at Saul and leaned forward, displaying an ample bust to its best advantage. 'Miss Hume was just checking out her travellers' cheques,' she told him chattily.

Candace was annoyed. The woman had no right to tell anyone what she was doing, but it was clearly useless to protest. Quite obviously had he asked for them the woman would have handed Candace's cheques over to him without demur.

'I see,' he said, and for a moment something cold and menacing moved into his eyes. It was gone so quickly that she decided she must have imagined it and when he said, 'I want to talk to you—shall we go and sit in those rather overstuffed chairs over there?' she allowed him to take her by the arm and lead her over to the foyer.

He relinquished her into the embrace of the chair, sat down himself and surveyed her enigmatically across a bowl of floating pink and cream frangipani flowers. The sweet scent, so evocative of the tropics, hung in the rapidly warming air. Even as she waited uneasily, someone touched a switch somewhere and the big ceiling fans began to pick up speed.

His eyes sharpened. 'Is something wrong?'

'No,' she said quickly. 'No, what could be wrong? Although I must admit I'm a little surprised to see you.'

'Oh, I came in to make sure that everything was settled with the chap who hires out the catamarans.'

She flushed, and said, 'I was going to do that. I must owe him something——'

'No, you paid him for the afternoon, he doesn't want anything more. The cat is back, so he hasn't lost anything.'

'Thank you,' she said stiffly.

He smiled. 'Thank me by coming out in the boat with me today,' he suggested.

The scent of the frangipani was stifling. Her eyes captured by his, Candace knew she looked stunned, her lips slightly parted.

'Just you?' she asked inanely.

'Yes, I'm afraid Stephanie has decided to stay on with the friends she's visiting.'

Her mind raced. Her first and strongest instinct was to grab the opportunity to form links with him so that she had a better chance of seeing his sister again, but caution warned her that he might not be so easy to hold off when they were alone on a boat together.

Her breath came a little faster. She said slowly, 'I don't think—I don't think it would be wise, Saul.'

He was watching her closely, his attention as weighty as a bruise on her soul. 'Why?' She bit her lip, and he resumed, 'I don't make a habit of leaping on women. If you're perturbed about that, let me assure you we won't be alone.'

'Gil?' she said huskily, hoping to avert his attention from the colour that streamed across her skin.

'Yes, Gil, as it happens. As well as being my driver he's an excellent boatman.'

No doubt billionaires took their bodyguards with them wherever they went. Although Saul didn't seem the sort of man who was afraid...

Her eyes drifted without volition across the muscular shoulders. He looked like a virile and lethal pirate in a pair of white cotton trousers and a loose red and white striped polo shirt, free, she was pleased to see, from emblems or writing. One of her irrational dislikes was people who felt impelled to wear slogans on their clothes.

Not for a moment did she think he had chosen the colour scheme to show off his teak tan, or the cut to reveal his heavily muscled arms and thighs. None of his clothes had the pristine look that might have suggested a layout in one of the glossy magazines; they were comfortably well worn. He looked dark and authoritative and casually tough. He looked, she thought with a subtly increasing heartbeat, absolutely fantastic.

When she became conscious of what she was doing she blushed again, and said quickly, 'I'd love to come out with you, thank you very much.'

'Good. Get into shorts and bring a cover-up of some sort,' he said briskly. 'The sun reflects back off the sea, and even in the shade you need to be well-protected.'

Ten minutes later she was back down in the foyer, clad in white shorts and a cotton Lycra bra top with a white muslin jacket and long trousers over them. She hoped fervently that he didn't think she had deliberately chosen garb to match his, but they were the only clothes she had that were suitable. Her hat was one she had bought the day after she had met them all in the market, a wide-brimmed plaited affair, and on her feet she wore white sandshoes. Large dark glasses hid much of her small face, providing some sort of protection from his penetrating gaze.

It was not, she had to admit as she snatched a look in the mirror before leaving her room, a glamorous outfit; she looked vaguely like a shepherd in a nativity play, or a masculine fairy swathed in muslin, but like the sunglasses it served as a form of armour.

Saul strode away from the reception desk as she came down the stairs, leaving the woman behind it flushed and laughing, but Candace saw the speculation in her face as her eyes followed them out into the hot street.

'I came in the boat,' he said casually, ignoring the interested glances of the passers-by. He didn't seem to notice that almost without exception women noted his intrinsic animal grace with admiring eyes, while men surveyed him with envy and respect. 'It's down at the docks.'

She nodded, not in the least surprised when the boat turned out to be the magnificent deep-sea fishing launch she had sailed around in the bay below his house; was it only yesterday afternoon?

As they walked along the wharf Gil said something to the three men he'd been talking to on the dock. They all nodded and moved away, grinning at her and Saul as they passed them. He seemed to know them, for he greeted them in the local dialect, but although she smiled Candace was very conscious of the curiosity in their faces as they looked at her. Did they think she was the latest of the beautiful women who had graced Saul Jerrard's boat, and ultimately his bed? Recalling Lydia Woolcott's perfect features and open sensuality, she decided they must be wondering what on earth had happened to Saul's taste.

Gil had moved to check the fenders at the stern. He too smiled at Candace, but she sensed his reservation, and wondered waspishly if he was going to make a dossier on her. Wasn't that what security men did? Well, he wouldn't find much in her life to speculate about. Most people would call it boring.

Saul went ahead, moving lithely as he swung over the edge of the wharf on to the teak decking of the huge cockpit. Turning, he extended his hands to Candace. She didn't want to take them, his touch did odd things to her thought processes, but something about his stance turned the gesture into a challenge, and with slightly heightened colour she put her hands in his and stepped down. Halfway down he caught her about the waist. The muscles in his arms and shoulders flexed as he lowered her gently. His hands lingered a moment before sliding up to her shoulders.

With a charm she guessed to be as fabricated as the amusement she saw in his eyes, he said, 'Welcome aboard, Candace.'

'Thank you,' she murmured.

Saul said, 'Come on, up to the flying bridge.' He nodded to Gil. 'I'll take her out. No, you don't need your bag up there, Candace, Gil will put it below when he's made sure we don't mark the hull if I hit the wharf.'

Gil grinned but said nothing as he went along to stand by the stern warp.

'Why is it three-storeyed?' Candace asked, staring up at the spectacular erection above the bridge.

Saul grinned. 'It's a tuna tower. It also helps stabilise the boat. The top tripod comes off when we go blue-water.'

'Where do you take her?'

He shrugged. 'I, unfortunately, very rarely get to take her anywhere. She goes to Cairns and the Bay of Islands in New Zealand for fishing, and I visit her.'

Candace looked around the comfortable seating in the flying bridge, the massive wheel and the impressive array of dials and gauges. Even more than his lovely house this rich man's toy, with its careless use of state-of-the-art technology in the service of sport, made her realise how very different the Jerrards were from her. The money that had been spent on this lovely thing would probably keep her for the rest of her life.

'You don't like it?' he said.

Damn, but she couldn't relax a moment. His alert wizard's eyes searched out her soul. Accepting this reaction for what it was—basic chemistry—meant admitting that she was attracted to the man. Well, of course she was, and her unwilling response to his blatant masculinity was making her ridiculously sensitive. The only thing she could do was to make sure that he didn't realise what was happening to her.

She smiled, a teasing, provocative little movement of her mouth. 'It would be profoundly ungrateful of me not to like it, wouldn't it?' she said. 'She's gorgeous.'

His answer was an ironic, humourless movement of his beautiful mouth as he turned away to the steering station. Put in her place, Candace watched silently as he manoeuvred the big boat away from the wharf so expertly that there was no need for Gil to use the fenders to protect the gleaming hull from damage. He stayed below while Saul took them across the small boat harbour, past a fascinating collection of yachts, from one massive great thing that looked as though its proper place was in the liner dock, to battered old-timers, some that bore registrations from as far away as London.

'Sea rovers,' Saul said.

She nodded, looking with interest at one that had a row of nappies fluttering along a line. It would be difficult to cope with a baby on board, but, oh, something about the idea of wandering the world in your own home attracted her powerfully.

She said as much, and they spent some time discussing the idea. He called it a wonderful fantasy, and was inclined to think it was a way of avoiding responsibilities. Just for fun, she argued against him. He knew what she was doing but she thought he enjoyed the discussion, and she set herself out to be entertaining, to get through the sparkling morning with finesse, using a lightly flirtatious manner as an armour.

He followed suit, although once or twice she had the nerve-racking feeling that he knew exactly what she was doing and why.

There was one very bad moment. He eased the engine back as they were passing one of the islands where the tourist boat had unloaded snorkellers, and Saul said casually, 'The coral is very pretty here, but you've seen it, haven't you?'

Agreement trembled on the tip of her tongue, then she remembered, and bit it back, feeling the shame heat her cheeks. Pretending not to hear, she had to turn away, for of course she had lied to him about it.

'No?' he drawled, after the silence had stretched out too long. 'Of course, I remember now, you told me you haven't been on the tourist trip. Ah, well, where we're going it's just as good.'

She nodded, hoping the skein of amber curls across her cheek hid the hot skin. He knows, she thought with a sudden panic, but when she plucked up the courage to look at him he gave a smile of such dazzling charisma that she forgot to look beyond it to his eyes.

After that he reverted back to being a provocative, amusing host, and she responded in kind. It wasn't difficult; the day was magnificent, the tropical heat tempered by a breeze, the view breathtaking, from the mountains in the interior brooding beneath shreds of cloud, to the sparkling waters of the bay. Saul took them on much the same track as the tourist boat, but they went further down the coast, while he pointed out places of interest along the way.

The big boat whipped smoothly through the water, on past the string of small islets that lay like feathery beads along the reef. On each grew coconut palms, their graceful heads inclining always towards the water.

When at last the changing note in the engine warned her that they were about to stop, it was late in the morning and they were heading smoothly towards one of the atolls. Gil came out from wherever he'd been and began to climb the ladder to the flying bridge.

Relaxed, laughing at an outrageous story Saul had just told her, Candace found herself thinking with surprise and pleasure that he was great fun, revealing in his anecdote a dry wit that could be cutting but was more often wryly tolerant of others' foibles and weaknesses.

*I could learn to like him very much,* she decided, and wondered why she should be so surprised at that. Her eyes scanned the little island, enjoying its isolation, its archetypal South Seas ambience. 'Oh, look!' she exclaimed, pointing. 'There's a house on it!'

As Gil came across to take the wheel Saul explained, 'It belongs to my cousin.'

She watched him stride across to the ladder. 'Where are you going?'

'To the top of the tuna tower to take her in through the coral.' He looked down at her. 'Want to come?'

For a moment she hesitated, but deep in the brilliant gaze turned on her there was speculation and a definite challenge. Her head came up. She nodded, and followed him up, arriving just as he took the wheel.

The railed platform was very small, and a long way from the deck, even further from the sea. Also, every slight sideways movement was magnified, so that although on the bridge the motion seemed almost non-existent, up there it swayed from side to side. A long way from side to side.

Her hands clamped on to the rail and she gulped. Saul's low laughter brought her head up. 'All right?' he asked.

She nodded firmly. He, of course, was standing easily, perfectly balanced, completely at home on the small, moving platform. Resentment simmered away inside her.

'Come and stand here beside me,' he coaxed, 'and keep an eye out for coral heads. We're going in through that deeper green passage. Look, there on the port side, you can see it snaking through the coral.'

'It doesn't look wide enough,' she said a little nervously.

'It is—just.' His teeth were white in a buccaneering smile.

She swallowed, watching carefully as he turned the wheel a little. 'Don't you have instruments to tell you where to go?'

'Yes, but they don't take the place of a sharp eye and a steady hand. Anyway, what's the pleasure in using instruments to do something when you can do it yourself?'

'If you thought that,' she said acidly, 'you'd never use a calculator or a car, or a boat like this, come to think of it.'

Not at all abashed, he grinned again. 'You're not watching. If we run aground I'll blame you.'

She turned her attention to the deep green passage winding through purple patches that revealed the frightening proximity of huge outcroppings of unforgiving coral, and began to give directions. Her sailing skills came back, so much so that when at last the anchor chain rattled down and the engines were cut she turned a triumphant face towards him.

'We got there,' she said, laughing a little, because the sharp edge of danger had excited her.

He bent and placed an expert kiss on her nose. 'Thank you.'

She stayed quite still, looking at him, her eyes wide and worried. Something had altered, something had changed; she didn't know what it was, but she knew that it was not a good thing. He scanned her face, his own oddly impassive, and then smiled teasingly. 'You look like a small animal,' he said. 'A dormouse, I think. Yes, a dormouse. Not a bit like a pirate intent on carving out her destiny in plunder and booty across the seven seas.'

Shaken, oddly hollow, she managed a light chuckle. 'It just goes to show how deceptive appearances are,' she said unevenly. 'Let's go down and take possession of this island. I could do with a bit of plunder and sacking.'

Gil had the inflatable dinghy out when they got to the cockpit, and was loading boxes and bins into it—enough, Candace thought, for an army.

'Gil has a large appetite,' Saul said, deadpan, when he caught her eyeing them.

The big man grinned, surprising her with the amusement, and the male affection she read in it. 'Got a lot to take care of,' he said cheerfully. 'Besides, Saul is not a delicate eater, either.'

The island was a little larger than most of the others but, like them, only a few feet higher than the water. Beneath the palms that were the only tall vegetation grew shiny-leaved shrubs, and coarse, pale grass, limp in the heat. The small house welcomed them, its wide wooden shutters open to the salty breeze, a low shrub with golden flowers growing around the shaded terrace. It was spare, and totally without luxury, but comfortable for all that.

'It's lovely,' Candace said, looking over the coconut matting on the floor and the hibiscus arranged in a glowing pile on a low table. 'Who lives here?'

'No one. Grant uses it as a retreat. In fact, I think he and his wife came here for their honeymoon.'

'You'd need to be very much in love,' Candace murmured, a note of cynicism flattening her tone.

Saul's voice was cool. 'You'd prefer the bright lights?'

Shrugging, she looked down to where Gil was taking the dinghy back to the boat. 'Let's just say I've never met a man I'd care to spend so much time alone with,' she said, refusing to be intimidated.

'Never been in love, Candace?'

Lightly she returned, 'Not even a schoolgirl crush. My problem is that I intend to like men, not fall for them.

I think something must have been left out of my character. Still, it makes for a nice peaceful life.'

'Oh, yes, this peaceful life you say you're so determined to achieve. Don't you want to get married, Candace, hear the prattling of small children at your knee?'

'The children, yes, I quite like children. But as for marriage——' She shook her head, her expression remote and a little mocking. 'Nope, not marriage. It seems more trouble than it's worth. People marry with such hope, such conviction that they're going to beat the statistics, yet a few years later most of them are bored to death with each other, even the ones who stay married—for the children's sake.' She pronounced the last few words with an odd intonation, almost of despair. 'So they separate in pain and malice, tearing the children apart, leaving them with no anchor, no security. If I ever get married it will be on the understanding that it lasts, ironclad, until the youngest child leaves home. And as there are very few men who'd sign a contract like that, I can't see myself marrying. It's no longer the sole reason for a woman's whole existence, you know.'

'Is that what happened to you?' he asked, his voice oddly gentle. 'Did your parents divorce?'

She produced a bleak little smile and moved away. 'Yes, a common enough story.'

'But a tragedy nevertheless,' he said.

Embarrassed, and angry with herself for giving something of herself away, she hunched a shoulder and went out into the sunlight. 'Isn't Gil coming back in?' she asked, looking out at the launch.

'He wants to do a bit of fishing,' he said smoothly. 'Do you want to eat now, or would you like to walk around the island?'

She gave him a hesitant smile, glad to see that his expression showed no signs that he was wondering about her outburst. 'It's not lunchtime yet. Let's walk around the island, and then we can go for a swim to work up an appetite.'

The sand crunched beneath their feet as he showed her shells in fabulous shades of pinks and creams and violets, seaweeds of fascinating designs, and bits of coral, pounded off the main reef by the merciless waves. He told her of the long, slow evolution of the reefs around volcanic islands, and how the huge atolls found in the Pacific were almost certainly the only signs left of volcanoes long since worn down by erosion and subsidence. He was fascinating, the deep flexible voice and sharp, subtle intelligence imbuing everything he spoke of with absorbing interest.

Candace forgot what she had come to Fala'isi to do, forgot everything but the pleasure of the moment, of walking like the first two people on the island, and listening to him in the languid atmosphere of this paradise.

After that they swam on the lagoon side of the atoll. Gil was still out in the dinghy, fishing with a line over the side some hundred yards or so from the shore.

'Does he ever catch anything?' Candace asked huskily, trying to blank out the strange jolt at the base of her spine when Saul casually stripped off his shorts to reveal black racing briefs that moulded the taut contours of his backside with loving and faithful precision.

He was beautifully made, the long, sleek muscles adding to the aura of strength and confidence that was as much part of him as the dark head of hair and the chiselled contours of his mouth.

She had pulled on a lime-green tank-suit, plain, unfussy; it had been the least startling bathing suit she could buy, although she had an uneasy suspicion that the smooth simplicity made a bit too much of her curves—a suspicion that was strengthened by the momentary flare of blue fire in Saul's eyes when he saw her in it. It was, however, perfectly decent, the scooped neck barely revealing the initial swell of her breast, the legs demurely cut, and the stark racing lines making it like a second skin in the water.

They donned masks and flippers and swam out across the coral, admiring the glowing little fish swarming through the reef in a fairyland of form and colours. Candace was touched by the way Saul kept a close eye on her until he accepted the fact that she knew what she was doing. As well as being arrogant, he was protective, which was anachronistic in the twentieth century, but vaguely—well, comforting. No one had protected her since she was ten, and of course she didn't need it; becoming dependent on anyone was the short route to weakness and pain. It had been a bitter lesson and not one she cared to repeat.

Stifling a treacherous instinct that whispered that it might be rather nice to have that solid strength to rely on now and again, she concentrated on the myriad patterns and delights in the water.

So intent was she on the theatre of activity beneath her that she gave a muffled exclamation when he said from close behind her, 'Time to go in, I think. Your back and shoulders are getting a little pink, and Gil's dancing around in the dinghy holding up a fish.'

Elated at the beauties of the reef, she lifted her head and pulled off the mask and snorkel, laughing. 'Oh, that was wonderful! If I could, I'd live here all the time!'

'Would you?' he said smoothly. 'Lotus-eating?'

She stood up and waded inshore, pulling a face at him. 'OK, so I'd get bored without something to do, but you must admit it's beautiful, out of this world.'

'Yes, I'm inclined to agree with you.' His eyes slipped down the pale length of her legs, touched like a lover's caress the feminine curves of breast and waist, slid across the arch of her hips in a survey that brought her out in goose-flesh.

An unbearable sensation of disquietude, a kind of fever in her blood, sang through her. Her eyes turned smoky and her breath locked in her throat. She felt that they were alone, enclosed in a bubble where the only realities were the silken caress of the water, and the dazzle of the sun, and the prison of his eyes, searching her soul.

Gruffly, she said, 'I'd better go and get dressed.'

They had Gil's fish for lunch, wrapped in banana leaves with limes and the cream from a couple of coconuts and baked over the embers of a fire. It was delicious, and Candace found herself relaxing again. The two men ate with every appearance of enjoyment, tossing idle comments back and forth. No one, Candace thought, would have taken them for employer and employee, but then no doubt to a billionaire his bodyguard was his best friend.

It was a peaceful scene. The subdued crackle of the fire as Gil added a piece of driftwood to the embers, the soughing of the breeze in the palms, the glitter of the sun on water and sand, and across the lagoon the blues and sharp greens, the dramatic purple crags and peaks of the main island, all added to the drowsy tropical atmosphere.

A small outrigger canoe swooped across the lagoon heading towards them, its brown sail and timeless design etching a pattern of endurance and agelessness. Gil got to his feet and watched it silently until it turned and headed off down towards the town.

Candace tried to imagine the sort of life Saul must lead, always at risk, and then somehow she was waking, to an amused suggestion from Saul that he carry her down to the dinghy.

'No,' she protested, struggling to open her eyes. 'No, I'm awake. I'm sorry, I had no idea—I wouldn't have gone to sleep... What time is it?'

'Time to go.' Saul was laughing, the sound unexpectedly tender on the languorous air. 'Come on, dormouse.'

She gave him a dazzled smile and, feeling an absolute fool, staggered to her feet, pushing her salty hair from her face. At least, she thought as she straightened, she had had the sense to put her muslin trousers and shirt on after she'd showered. Armour she had thought it to be, and armour it certainly was, shielding her from prying eyes as well as the too vigorous caress of the sun.

Crumpled and grubby, she allowed herself to be packed away as efficiently as the left-overs, and it wasn't until they were halfway across the lagoon that she realised they were not headed towards Fala'isi town.

A stupid, unwarranted pang of fear held her motionless for a moment. She said, 'Where are we going?'

'Back to the house.' Saul smiled at her. 'It's easier if we go straight back, instead of getting tangled up with the rush hour at the docks. Everyone heads off home round about this time. If I can't coax you into having dinner with us I'll take you home.'

'Us' he said, so Stephanie must be waiting, or on the way back. She said dismally, 'I'm in no fit state to have dinner with you or anyone else.'

'Oh, you can shower back at the house.' He paused, then added deliberately, 'And what's wrong with the sarong you wore last night? I'm no expert, but it seemed to me to suit you very well.'

She shot him a quick suspicious look, but there seemed no ulterior meaning behind the comment, so she relaxed, allowing herself to be persuaded.

Only Stephanie was not there this time either. Apparently she had rung during the day to say that she was staying one more night, and would Saul collect her the next morning? Candace felt a profound disappointment, but mingled with it was an uneasy anticipation. She had thoroughly enjoyed her day on the water, but although Gil had been discreet he had always been there.

Slowly it occurred to her that the intense compulsion which had fuelled her quest for the last three years had altered in direction. She refused to admit it, but as she showered and climbed back into the sarong—newly washed and pressed—that she had worn the day before, she accepted that it was Saul who was taking Stephanie's place in her mind, becoming the object of her interest.

It was not that her need to find Stephanie was any the less; it was just that another aim was becoming stronger. The more she learnt of Saul, the more she wanted to know. He fascinated her, absorbed her, intrigued her in a way that no man ever had before.

The evening was a repeat of the one before, but she thought they were more at ease with each other, more relaxed. Until after dinner, when she sat with him in the big sitting-room with its split-cane blinds rolled up and the stars and moon glimmering on the lush vegetation, and listened to the earthshaking intensity of Mahler's Second Symphony.

# CHAPTER FIVE

FLUSHING, Candace realised that she was staring at Saul with total absorption, her eyes caught and held by a force of will she couldn't resist. Her lips formed a word, the meaning of which she had no idea, but he smiled in insolent triumph, and she saw the satisfaction in his eyes.

It didn't warm them. Had anything ever warmed them? Passion, delight, pleasure—or even then did they blaze with that fiercely cold fire?

He said nothing, but she rose and came to him as though she were sleep-walking, her eyes dilated and glittering in the dim light, her mouth soft and red and sensuous. He was sitting in a huge chair with white cushions, stark against the darkness of his shirt and the trousers that clung to his lean legs and hips. An ankle rested on the opposite knee; in any other man but Saul the pose would have struck her as affected, but Saul made it entirely natural. As she came up to him he lowered his leg and leaned back in the chair.

A tiny spasm of common sense penetrated through her thralldom. She stopped, but he caught her hand and urged her within the framework of his legs, his knees closing to hold her prisoner. Fear struggled with a wild excitement she had never experienced before.

Every instinct save one urged her to flee, but that one, more basic and stronger than all the rest, held her still. Through flickering lashes she looked down into his hard, handsome, confident face, resenting him, wanting all sorts of impossible things with him, terribly afraid that she was in too deep, that she was never going to climb out of the pit her weakness and his dark magnetism had dug.

This, she thought bleakly, this was what had been building ever since she saw him across the restaurant floor.

He didn't move, not a muscle, merely watched her watching him, that small smile of satisfaction tucking the corners of his beautiful mouth as though he knew all he had to do was hold out his hand, and she was his.

She had a horrible feeling that he was right.

In a voice husky with suppressed longing, she said, 'That's some look. How long did you have to practise before you got it right?'

Sheer astonishment wiped the smug little smile from his mouth, but she wasn't able to enjoy his confusion for long. The lean hand wrapped loosely around hers tightened; she was drawn down on to his lap, one of his hands sliding inexorably up her arm, the other clamping around her waist. She looked up into those cold eyes, glittering with an impersonal passion, and saw them fixed on to her mouth.

Heat flashed along her veins, leaping like a firestorm from cell to cell throughout her body. Frightened now, she began to struggle, but that cruel, beautiful mouth crushed her protests to nothingness in a kiss that sent her senses reeling into confusion.

He was merciless, ravaging her lips with hard ferocity, then softening into a seductive languor that relaxed all her fears but the most basic, that of losing herself in an addiction against which she had no defences.

'Open your mouth,' he ordered softly against her trembling lips. 'Open for me. I've been wanting to taste you ever since I saw you.'

She lifted heavy eyelids; his own were lowered, the thick, straight lashes shielding the spellbinding penetration of his eyes.

Her tongue stole out to dampen her lips, and the tiny movement was betrayal enough. As though she had surrendered something rare and precious, he smiled and lowered his head again, his importunate mouth seducing hers open until he could slide through into the sweet depths.

Something primeval shuddered down her spine, set off a fire in the pit of her stomach, slow and sweet and honeyed, backed by a terrible urgency. Her arms slid slowly up, her hands curling into the fine material of his shirt. Beneath them his heart hammered, blending with the heavy thudding of hers until there was no distinction between them. His mouth was slow and thorough, exploring, probing, making him master of all her responses. She had always hated this kind of kissing, feeling smothered by it, but Saul was an expert, and she realised now why it was considered so erotic.

Desire hummed in the air around them, golden, mindless, a restless imperative that overrode the warnings of heart and mind in a flood of savage compulsion. She wanted to know—after all this time she wanted to know what it was like to lie with a man, this man, to yield to him all the secret hidden places of her body, surrender and be taken in the most primitive way there was. Frighteningly aware of her own needs, the clamour in her blood, the aching in her body, she recognised the primal yearning for completion.

His hand came slowly up from her waist to touch her breast. She froze, and he lifted his head and said softly, 'I've never had to practise it, Candace.'

'Practise what?' Weighted lids almost hiding dazed eyes, she watched his mouth move as he answered.

'The look. It comes naturally when I look at you.'

The smooth words belied the painful hammering of his heartbeats. A strange pang tore deep inside her body, because he was lying.

How odd that she should be able to read him so well. There was no alteration to his tone, none of the hidden subliminal signs that point to deception; he was a consummate actor, the complete professional, yet she sensed the reservation in him. This was a calculated experiment.

'I don't believe you,' she said, her voice slow and husky, her brain only just working.

'You don't believe that I want you?' His chest lifted in a silent breath. 'I wanted you the first time I saw you. I could feel your eyes on me all the way across the room, but when I got close you looked down at your plate, oh, so modestly, and all I could see was your lashes, thick and dark against skin like ivory satin, and a red mouth. Then when we met in the market, after you fainted you opened eyes like grey crystals, warm and clear and sparkling. Diamonds and satin, with silken hair and a mouth like a soft red flower—the textures of sensuality, of desire. Oh, wanting doesn't even begin to describe how I feel about you, Candace.'

His breath on her cheek was warm. She thought of the storms spawned in these regions that occasionally found their way to New Zealand, tumultuous cyclones of wind and rain, of destruction, and shuddered. Like a hurricane, Saul was capable of damage beyond her imaginings.

It took all of her will-power to pull away; although he made no effort to stop her, the lure of his scent, male-potent and infinitely attractive, the lean hardness of his body against her more yielding flesh, the fine-grained texture of his skin, all combined to form a powerful reason for letting him do whatever he wanted with her.

Now she understood, she realised wearily, why her adoptive parents had chosen others over her. Not that she could desert a child, not ever, but those moments in his arms revealed why physical passion was one of the mightiest influences in the world. It had brought down kingdoms, ruined lives, led to the downfall of dynasties and religions; it was a power that once unharnessed was as fierce as the most vicious tropical hurricane.

Yet there had to be some sort of defence against it; reason and logic had power also. It was this thought that finally dragged her to her feet and took her more or less steadily across the room. He let her get to the door before he spoke.

'Candace.'

She stopped, but did not turn.

His voice was indolent, smooth as cream yet rendered complex by an undertone of determination that lifted the hairs on the back of her neck. 'Candace, I intend to have you. One night I'm going to discover all your secrets, make myself master of everything you have, everything you are.'

His cool assumption that she was his for the taking infuriated and terrified her. Her mind went completely blank. She drew a deep breath into lungs that hurt and retorted stiffly, 'I don't want——'

He came up behind her in a silent lunge, turning her with cruel hands and forcing her face up so that he could read it. His face was darkly etched with some intense emotion. There was something wild in that stare, something tense and predatory, as his eyes swept her in a swift, crackling survey.

Electricity sparked between them as he said in an even voice, 'I assume you know just how that sulky, wilful mouth, those half-closed eyes, act on most men. I'm no exception. I want to see what is hidden behind those lashes, kiss that mouth until it opens in desperation for me.'

Her lashes flew upright. He was watching her with such hunger in his eyes that she cried out, a soft little sound that seemed to snap the control he had been exerting.

But his mouth was not ravenous. Very lightly, he touched the hollow in her throat where her pulse beat like a trapped bird. Her breath fought for ingress, but she only managed to drag enough air into her fainting lungs to keep her conscious, so that she could endure this fine, searing torture.

Yet he was not hurting her. He was not even holding her tightly. So why couldn't she get away?

She drew in another ragged breath, then moaned silently as his tongue touched the warm skin of her throat. 'So fragile,' he taunted softly, turning his head to bite gently at the exact spot where her neck met her shoulder. 'You're like a pearl, soft and smooth and gleaming, rare and precious enough to drive men to kill so that they can hold it in their hands and claim ownership. Beautiful as moonlight, and just as dangerous; worth a man's soul, a man's honour and pride.'

Shudders of sensation were crawling down her spine, up from her toes, jagging out from the place where his teeth tenderly savaged her skin. She couldn't stop the high, wild little sound that broke from her, and he laughed, and turned her slightly.

The knot at her breast was brushed aside, the fine cotton sliding like a lover's caress over the pale skin beneath, followed by his hand, dark against white, travelling with sure direction to cup her breast. She gasped, her mouth trembling, her body shaking with the exquisite pang that ran through her. Her breasts were heavy, almost painful, and as she stared into the dark, implacable face she felt something happening to the nipples, a kind of tightness, a drawing sensation.

'See, your body knows,' he said harshly. 'It can't lie, Candace. Now try to convince yourself you don't want me.'

She could only stare at him, bewildered by the betrayal, swamped by sensations that ate into her bones, a cruel, biting hunger that needed something...

She gasped, and gasped again as he took her breast into her mouth, suckling gently at first, and then more fiercely, before releasing the throbbing tip to kiss the pale flesh close by, pushing up her lush roundness so that he could feast his eyes on it.

'You make me want things I've never even heard of,' he said deeply. 'I have to have you...'

The stark declaration of desire shocked her out of the golden tide of fire that had wrapped her in dizzying sensuality. She lifted dazed eyes, read the fierce feral hunger etched into the predator's features. Her skin tightened. She looked away, and her mind saw herself, half naked, trembling, mouth softly drooping with desire, her form pliant and willing.

'No,' she stammered, jerking herself free.

He didn't come after her. She couldn't breathe as he fought down the primal urge, fought the need that was riding him and won. Something ugly moved in the depths of his eyes.

Pressing a hand to her chest, she jerked the material across to cover her nakedness, her hand shaking with adrenaline and reaction. Her tongue touched dry lips. She whispered, 'I can't. I won't. Please.'

Her shoulders held so rigidly that they hurt, she backed off, unable to break free from the prison of his gaze. Heat snaked through her. Dazedly, she thought she could feel his hunger, weighing down on her so that she couldn't think. Even as she wavered she realised that any surrender would reduce her to a slave of sensations and needs so primal they were deeply dangerous. This mindlessness, this overwhelming impulse to yield to the passion that sizzled about them like an aura, this was what she had spent a lifetime fearing. And he had only to look at her to set up the forbidden vibrations deep inside her traitorous body.

Opening her eyes, she turned abruptly away. 'I'm not prepared to take Lydia's place,' she said harshly. 'And I don't want a light flirtation either.'

Braced, she waited for his reply.

He demanded silkily, 'Why?'

It was not the first time she had had to deal with such an attitude. Many men thought that freedom meant licence, that when a woman was attracted to a man bed was the next logical step. Once she had even tried to explain to an impatient boyfriend why she was cautious, only to be given a lecture on contraception! Since then she had always kept things light, offering friendship and affection only, and when they wanted more she left them with few pangs.

But this man . . . She struggled for an answer he would accept, then chose the easiest way out. 'Because I don't sleep with strange men,' she said bluntly. 'I don't know you.'

'But you want me.' He said it softly, his eyes as keen as daggers as they surveyed her face, the blazing blue almost swallowed up by darkness.

She shrugged, forcing her voice to steadiness. 'So what? It happens all the time. It needn't mean anything.'

He didn't like that. His mouth hardened as he said, 'Or perhaps I've missed out something of vital importance?' When she stared at him he added deliberately, 'I can promise you won't lose by it.'

She looked at him for a tense, scorching moment before returning with a contempt she didn't try to hide, 'I suppose I should have expected that. No, Mr Jerrard, I don't want your money. What I want isn't yours to give, and I'll get it myself by my own efforts.'

It took her two steps to reach the door and she should have made it, but even as she stepped through his hands held her back.

'Let me go,' she said tonelessly.

He turned her to face him, his grip gentle yet inexorable. She held her head high, meeting his gaze with all the composure she could muster, her soft lips folded into a tight painful line.

'My mistake,' he said smoothly, those incredible eyes searing her skin as they searched her face. 'Candace, look at me.'

She lifted her lashes, giving him a deadly level stare from pupils dilated into darkness, asking no quarter, giving none. He smiled, and she thought wildly that it was perhaps the first time he had allowed her to see his real emotions. A lean hand touched her brow where it winged out towards her hairline, his finger smoothing the dark line with something like tenderness.

'Shall we start again?' he suggested, dropping his hand and looking gravely at her.

This approach was harder to deal with than the blazing sensuality, profoundly disturbing because it seemed to her that beneath the surface regret he was watching her with a cool analytical appraisal to see how she reacted to the buttons he was pushing.

Mirrors, she thought, made incoherent by confusion and frustration. He was working sleight of hand with mirrors, dazzling her, jamming all the signals given by her senses so that she didn't know what he was doing.

Stiffly she returned, 'There's nothing to start.'

His smile was slow and warm and amused, even a little teasing. 'If that's the way you want things, that's the way they'll be. I'd like you to see a little more of Stephanie, if you can be bothered. She's young and bored, and as she's convalescing she can't be her usual active self. She talked quite a bit about you after you'd met. You did like her, didn't you?'

Her lashes quivered, and sank beneath his piercing glance. This was the chance she had longed for, and she wasn't going to turn it down, not now, not when she was so near to her goal.

Mind made up, she ignored the instinct that told her it would be dangerous to get too close to him, and said quietly, 'I—yes. Yes, I liked her.'

His hand tightened on her shoulder, then dropped away. Smiling, his expression bland, he said lazily, 'Good.' And before she had time to step away he bent his head and kissed her, a fleeting, impersonal brush of firm lips over hers, yet it sent the blood screaming through her body in a clamour of sensation that warned her how wise she had been to turn him down.

It was like a reprieve from hell, a stay of execution. She drew a deep breath but before she could speak he said, 'I'll take you back.'

Her tongue seemed too big to fit her mouth but she managed to say, 'I'll be all right. I'll get a taxi.'

'I won't leap on you, I promise. Clearly I got the wrong signals. I apologise. All right?'

Slowly, enormous eyes fixed on his face, she nodded.

Half an hour later she was breathing more easily in her motel room. All the way back he had been as courteous and pleasant as though those maddened minutes in his arms had never happened; perhaps for him they hadn't. Perhaps he was able to ignore such occasions because to him they weren't important.

Yet he had seemed to mean the words that were scorched into her brain; his voice had been raw with suppressed emotion. At that moment, she was sure, he had wanted her. Perhaps, she thought dismally, he was able to cut himself off from his passions without difficulty, repressing them with the icy control of the truly unemotional. Perhaps passion was not something he valued much. A case of familiarity breeding contempt?

She didn't sleep. Frustration ached through her, taunting her with images, teasing her with unfulfilled desires. Towards morning she gave up, and went to sit in the window, watching the sky slowly lighten above the reef while she tried very hard not to think. She welcomed the dawn with a fervour that had something of desperation in it. At least she could do something in the daylight hours, look at things to take her mind off what had happened the night before. And some time today there would be Stephanie.

That prospect was enough... It had to be enough.

She swam in the pool, then showered and hid the evidence of a wakeful night with skilfully applied cosmetics before she went out on to the motel terrace for breakfast. Not hungry, she forced herself to eat papaw with passion-fruit pulp squeezed over it, and creamy yoghurt followed by coffee that tasted better than any wine she had ever savoured. Close to the equator as Fala'isi was, the air could never be crisp, but in the mornings it was balmy, with the lambent promise of a languid afternoon and an evening of dark velvet.

She was still enjoying her second cup of coffee when one of the waitresses came out, smiling, and said, 'Miss Hume, there's someone waiting for you at Reception.'

It was Saul, casually clad in jungle-green trousers and a paler shirt. 'I thought you might like to come with me to pick Stephanie up from Chapman's,' he said.

She hesitated, but of course she wanted to go. 'Yes. I'd like that,' she replied a little stiffly.

'Good.'

'I'll change...'

He smiled at her, teasingly, with the charm she suspected so much, his eyes glinting with laughter. 'No, you look fine just the way you are,' he said.

She raised her brows, for the sunny pale lemon dress was nothing spectacular, but went obediently with him, her bag clutched tightly in her hand.

The road wound its way through the narrow streets and then was suddenly out of the town, purring past the greenish-yellow shade cast by banana plantations as they left the coast and began to climb towards the volcanic interior of the island. Well-paved but narrow, it carried a lot of other traffic, most of which walked or rode heavily laden bicycles, as well as an assortment of livestock that seemed afflicted with a death wish. When the fourth lot of scrawny chickens had run shrieking and flapping their wings to the refuge of the roadside, Candace couldn't prevent a low chuckle.

The man beside her, driving with skill and a nice judgement of what each animal was likely to do, observed, 'It's worse at night. Pigs sleep in the dust on the side of the road, and the headlights scare hell out of them. They wake disorientated so they tend to blunder across in front of any approaching vehicle. And there's nothing like a pig to do untold damage to a car.'

'I don't suppose it's terribly good for the pig, either,' she returned tartly.

His teeth were a sudden flash of white in his face. 'Pigs are virtually indestructible. I've seen one emerge from a fracas that destroyed two cars and several bicycles, and take itself, snorting indignantly, to the side of the road apparently none the worse for wear.'

The picture he evoked made her laugh, a soft, irresistible sound. 'Even so, it's less traumatic than London traffic. The first time I saw an intersection in the West End I almost passed out from culture shock. Fortunately I arrived in London first, so the greater free-for-alls in Paris and Rome were not quite so horrifying.'

His shoulders moved in a slight shrug. 'Almost anything is preferable to the traffic in a big city.'

Yet he looked the archetype of a sophisticated urban man, unfazed by anything a city could throw at him. She couldn't prevent the swift sideways assessment of her eyes, but blushed when for a fraction of a second they met the narrowed blue fire of his.

Embarrassed by the swift smile that didn't soften his hard mouth, she turned her head to gaze out of the window. A village came into sight, tucked into a hollow above a stream, the high-pitched thatched roofs of the huts entirely appropriate in the drowsy tropical landscape. The gardens were immaculately tidy; in one she saw a woman desultorily sweeping the grass with a bunch of twigs. Each house was surrounded by hibiscus and other flowering bushes and low hedges of croton plants, with their brilliant pink and gold and crimson leaves. It made an exotic picture, so alien to the prim villages of the old world and the raw-boned settlements in Australia and New Zealand. Again she recalled those sailors of the eighteenth century who thought they had discovered paradise.

'You enjoyed your holiday in Europe?' he asked casually.

Absorbed in the sights and sounds of Polynesia, she nodded absently. 'Loved it. It was like a homecoming.'

'How long were you there?'

'A year.'

'And what exactly did you do there?'

She shrugged. 'This and that,' she said, deliberately vague. 'A lot of sightseeing.' Most of it done from the seat of a bicycle, but she wasn't going to tell him that, or that she spent each night in youth hostels. Saul Jerrard was very definitely accustomed to travelling in comfort, and the very best hotels, names familiar even to those who lived on the other side of the world. Admittedly, so far he'd shown little evidence of snobbishness, but she wasn't going to give him any ammunition.

They were climbing, crossing the spine of the island, threading their way slowly through steeper and steeper hills. The mountains ahead were green and fierce and jagged, and even on a day as hot and fine as this there was mist veiling the ferocious peaks, occasionally thinning to reveal gasping plunges into chasms thousands of feet below.

'When you look at these hills, it's no wonder most of the old gods were cruel,' Saul said calmly, then, uncannily echoing her thoughts of a few minutes ago, 'This is the other side of paradise. The darker side.'

Candace couldn't repress a tiny shudder as a cold breath of some nameless emotion crawled across her skin.

'Doesn't your cousin live on the coast?' she asked, watching the suicidal leap of a waterfall from a notch in a jagged crag to the floor of the valley.

He swung the wheel off the main road and up a narrow rutted track. The big car took it easily, its springs unprotesting. 'He does. However, I thought you might like to see what the interior is like. Unless these roads worry you? Do you suffer from vertigo?'

'No,' she said, settling back into the seat. And she trusted his driving implicitly, but she wasn't going to tell him that.

However, this road was enough to test her resolution, winding up a narrow, deserted valley before edging along the top of a precipice, always climbing, inching on.

'This is the old trail across the island,' he told her absently as they crept around a hairpin bend. The road widened a little and he pulled the car on to the side and stopped the engine. 'There, hop out and have a look.'

Up here it was cooler, the air more fresh, carried by a steady breeze. Candace breathed deeply and walked across the road to a narrow area that had been turned into a look-out, with picnic seats and table, and a railing at the edge of the cliff. In such a wild landscape the ordinary artefacts of western civilisation looked absurd.

It was very quiet. She stood still as Saul came over the road to stand beside her, gazing down into an awe-inspiring abyss. The joyous catherine wheels of tree-ferns showed up brilliantly all the way down the cliff. Between brilliant green taro patches in the valley below, a narrow thread of stream wound its way towards the sea. Waterfalls were streaks of silver, their water collecting in clouds of mist as they dashed themselves to silver shards against the cliffs.

'It's all green,' she said softly, wonderingly. 'Even the cliffs are covered in greenery.'

'Yes. It's like no other place on earth.'

She turned slightly, looking out beyond the wild crags and huge spears of rock that stabbed the sky, to the lush greenery of the coastal plains and still further on to the lagoon, in all the myriad hues from blue to green, fading into a mysterious purple where a cloud shadow moved across the water, and in the distance cut off by the white line of the reef that separated it from the limitless breadth of the Pacific Ocean. Smaller islands lay in a cluster a few miles away, blue-violet, beckoning with the siren's lure of the unknown.

Something blocked her throat; she said on a whisper, 'I know why the first Europeans here thought they had found paradise.'

'A paradise they proceeded to despoil and ruin,' he said harshly. 'It happens even now; the Pacific peoples want only to live in peace, but other powers export their own shabby conflicts, trying to involve the indigenous people in their nasty, messy little wars, their alien philosophies and aims.'

She looked up, caught a strange look on his face and, even as she turned, felt a jab in her neck. Her hand lifted, then fell, and her last thought was a wail of betrayal into the darkness.

She woke with a thudding head and a dry mouth, dry-retching, her mind blank and woolly. She was lying on her stomach on a hard bed; when the spasm had passed she said thinly, 'Mum?'

No one answered, although she knew someone was there. She could feel a presence behind her, but as her mind gave up the struggle and she slipped into sleep she knew that there was no mother to soothe away her hurts, hadn't been for years.

It was dark when she woke again, and this time she remembered what had happened, more or less. Her mouth still felt as though she hadn't drunk for a century, but the ache in her head had receded to a dull throb, and the nausea was gone. She just felt empty and weak, lax as a doll without stuffing.

She didn't open her eyes. As soon as she did that she would have to accept the monstrous thing that had happened to her, and she didn't feel strong enough yet. She lay still, listening to the sounds. There was water, a liquid sweetness that denoted a small stream flowing over rocks, and the quiet call of a dove, soothing and soft. And slowly, inevitably, the soft sibilance of someone breathing.

Panic clawed at her with ferocious fingers. She remembered Saul's scenario. 'Let's say that I kidnap you and take you off to a love-nest up in the mountains,' he had said, 'and there have my evil way with you...'

Surely he hadn't...? Her whole mind rejected the supposition. She just could not believe that he would go to those extremes to rape someone as ordinary as Candace Hume. Not when he must know that a little more pressure would find her in his bed in spite of her vehement protestations!'

She drew a deep, ragged breath. Think! she adjured herself. Why would he see you as some sort of threat?

He said, 'Candace.' And when shock held her still, 'I know you're awake.'

Slowly, her mind rebelling as though by refusing to face the issue she could make it untrue, she lifted her heavy eyelids. The light split through her head; she bit back a moan and let her lashes fall again.

But he was merciless. 'Come on, wake up.'

Faced by a will superior to her own, she opened her eyes, her brow furrowed and painful, her mouth trembling as she whispered, 'You swine.'

'I'm sorry,' he said almost indifferently. 'I know you feel like hell, but it will be over soon.'

He was still dressed in the clothes he had worn when he picked her up, but she was lying naked under a thin covering. Sweat crawled sluggishly across her skin. Shivering, she swallowed and said thickly, 'What have you done to me?'

'Nothing, beyond stripping you. And that was done as quickly as possible. I promise you I didn't touch you in any intimate way.'

No, he had only handled her body. No doubt he had removed her clothes as quickly, deftly and impersonally as he had made love to her.

Nausea made her gag. He got up and went over to a table by the door, coming back with a glass of water. 'Here, drink this,' he ordered.

She didn't want to, but he slid his arm behind her head and lifted it, holding the glass to her lips. Sensing that he would tip it down her throat if she tried to refuse it, she drank. Besides, her throat was on fire. When it was all gone he put the glass on to the floor and sat down in a chair beside the bed, his eyes fixed on her face.

Ignoring him, she grimaced as she gingerly looked around. The room was dark but she could see enough to discern walls and a shuttered window, a floor of pale tiles, and the single bed she was lying on. It was impersonal, without pictures or ornaments, without curtains or lamps or mats.

It looked like a cell, she thought with a disconcerting jolt of panic in her midriff. Without volition she whispered, 'Why have you done this?'

'I think you know why,' he said after a pause during which he seemed to be making up his mind, 'and if you don't, then it's better that you don't.'

Before she had time to assimilate this non-answer, he turned and walked towards a door.

'Wait,' she croaked frantically, attempting to sit up. Her head whirled hideously and she sank back down again.

'What is it?'

'What's going to happen to me?'

His voice altered. 'Nothing. There's a bathroom through the door there, and you'll be fed when you're hungry. Just lie there and recover.'

She opened her eyes to the soft sound of the door closing. Completely alone, she sank back into sleep.

It was dark when she woke again, but a light gleamed through the half-open door that she had noticed just before she slept. Assailed by an urgent need, she managed to get up off the bed and make her unsteady way across to it, welcoming the coolness of the tiles beneath her feet. The bathroom was small and basic, with bars on the window and a screen that prevented her from seeing out.

She washed her hands and her face and neck then used her cupped hands to drink from. Her head, she was relieved to discover, was no longer throbbing, but it felt thick. Thought was difficult, and she wondered with a sick alarm whether he had given her anything to slow her down.

Hideous tales of various drugs whirled in her brain; she banished them. Naturally she would feel a slight case of terminal confusion until whatever drug he had used to knock her out was gone from her system.

Slowly, her fingers sought the place at the side of her throat where she had felt the quick pain. Her frown deepened; there didn't seem to be anything there, not even a lump. But that period of unconsciousness had certainly been artificial.

Why?

The question throbbed through her brain. She could come up with no answer, no reason for this to have happened to her. He couldn't possibly know why she wanted to make contact with Stephanie, could he? Her fear took her by surprise. She had never known that it could be like a blow to the stomach, making her feel sick and shaky.

She rattled the handle, calling Saul's name, and stood tensely, waiting for him to come back, to laugh and say that the door must have stuck, to give her a reasonable explanation. But there was no answer, no easy, reasonable solution to the situation she was in.

Anger strengthened her arm. She jerked at the handle, but it was strong and didn't budge. Why on earth did a bedroom door need such a lock? Panting slightly, she ran back across the room to the shutters, and examined the lock there. It too was strong, a deadbolt that needed a key to open it all times, and the shutters were solid, impossible to break.

Slowly, her eyes dilated, a hand held to her trembling mouth, she turned to gaze with unseeing eyes around the room that was now her prison.

A soft little sound broke from her, but she swallowed and walked upright across to the narrow bed, sitting down to hold her head in her hands.

Why?

All sorts of hideous possibilities whirled around in her brain, but she could give credence to none of them. Common sense rejected the possibility of his being involved in white slavery. Then why was she locked here? He knew that no one was waiting for her to return; she bit her lip painfully as she cursed the naïveté with which she had given facts away. He must have been trying to find out what she would be likely to do.

But why?

Saul seemed far too normal to indulge in the more esoteric aspects of perversity that would entail her imprisonment; but how well did she know him, really? Did he get some perverted sexual pleasure from terrorising women?

Panic rose in a black flood inside her, so that she whimpered, closing her eyes in rejection. Ruthlessly she forced it back. She was being ridiculous; she might have little idea of what made a man tick, but she was willing to wager her life on the fact that Saul was not a sadist. Ruthless, yes; but twisted? No.

Which meant that he had what seemed to him to be a good reason for imprisoning her.

Pain squeezed her heart in a giant vice. Now, at last, she knew why Saul Jerrard, billionaire and brilliant, sophisticated man of the world, had found Candace Hume interesting. Not because he wanted her; no, he had used her hopeless attraction to bring her here because he suspected something of her.

Her brain was working furiously. Had he known that she'd deliberately engineered that first meeting?

That would explain why Stephanie had been absent for the last two days. Whisked out of harm's way. And, of course, if Saul's suspicions had been roused by the mock faint then her arrival at the house the next day would have set that clever brain really going.

But this—this kidnapping was an over-reaction, surely?

She hid her face in her shaking hands.

After a while she realised that her hands were clasped so tightly together they were sore. Easing them apart, she watched with empty eyes as the blood surged painfully beneath the skin.

Supposing, her brain whispered, supposing he doesn't intend you to survive?

She couldn't face this. It was totally beyond her comprehension. Stiffly she lay back on the bed, trying to remember just what he had said to her, but her brain whirled into meandering repetitions, and before she realised it she was asleep again.

When she woke again it was early in the morning, just before dawn, she thought, as she lay listening to the call of the tikau birds singing their exquisite duet. A wry, haunted smile hurt her lips. So much for the legendary qualities of the song! It seemed highly unlikely that she was going to meet her lover in the next twelve months!

But at least the night's sleep had dispelled the last fumes of the drug, and, although she felt tired and boneless, she was able to think again. Sleep had also put to rest her fear that Saul intended to kill her. He might be a ruthless man—well, the events of the last twenty-four hours had proved that he was—but she didn't think he was murderous, or twisted. She didn't know why, but she was sure he had to have what seemed to him an overwhelming reason for kidnapping her and imprisoning her wherever this was.

She just wished she knew what it was.

This time when she emerged from the bathroom a tray had been left on the floor inside the door. Her appetite had returned with a rush and she checked out the food eagerly, draining a large glass of fruit juice before she sat on the side of the bed with the thin sheet wrapped around her and ate muësli and fruit, and bacon and eggs. There was no coffee or tea, but that didn't matter because as soon as she had eaten she was overcome with tiredness again, and only had time to put the tray on to the floor and huddle into the bed before she fell asleep once more.

He had given her a sedative. She woke with the thought in her mind, not consciously thinking it, just knowing that it was true. In the fruit juice.

# CHAPTER SIX

SHEER spontaneous outrage held Candace rigid in the narrow bed. Anger, she had discovered, was a lot easier to deal with than fear; it even drove it out, so that she wasn't paralysed by that sick panic.

From now on she would have to drink from the tap in the bathroom, catching the water in her cupped hands. Tears squeezed from beneath her lids as the vivifying anger seeped away to be replaced by hopelessness, a profound sense of abandonment and betrayal. She was wallowing in self-pity, her mind told her sternly. Being totally wimpish.

Lunch was delivered as she dozed on the bed; she heard the slight movements as the tray was put down but before she could rouse herself her gaoler had gone. It was salad and an omelette, superbly cooked, and there was another jug of orange juice with it. Eyeing the jug balefully, she forced herself to eat the food, then emptied the juice down the handbasin in the bathroom.

Saul came noiselessly in just as she was emerging from the bathroom with the empty jug in her hand.

She had draped the sheet around her like a sari; it made walking difficult but at least it was better than being naked. When she saw him standing inside the door, dark as Lucifer in the small bare room, his eyes narrowed and intent as they swept from the jug to her guilty face, and back again, something snapped.

Without thinking she drew back her hand and flung the jug at him, narrowly missing his face as he ducked out of the way. Before he had time to move any further she flew across the room and launched herself at him,

110

her arms swinging wildly as she tried one of the sure-fire methods of disabling a man, her knee coming up with vicious, mindless force.

He moved like a cat, swift and deadly and without thought for her smallness, his hands clamping on to her shoulders, jerking her feet out from underneath her as he flung her on to the bed, and then landing on her with such precision that the breath whumped out of her in a noisy, painful exhalation.

Sheer determination kept her going, even though the breath she drew hurt like barbed wire in her lungs. With lips drawn back in a snarl she fought savagely, furiously, her sense of betrayal and a bitter, bleak pain combining to give her unnatural strength. Her teeth fastened on to his shoulder and he swore, his cruel hand forcing her head back until her throat strained in a painful arc; she sobbed as his forearm settled painfully across it, cutting off her air. Her lips moved without sound; in her pale face her eyes blazed black as jet, lit from behind by fires of outrage.

'Stop it!' The words came from between his teeth. He lifted the hard bar of his forearm a fraction and she gasped for air, dragging it into her tortured lungs. Mercilessly his arm came back down again, but not quite so hard; pressed back into the mattress she lay sullenly quiescent, struggling for breath.

'Right,' he said, still in that deadly voice. 'Let's have the answers to a few questions, shall we? Why are you here?'

'Because you bloody well brought me here.'

'On Fala'isi.' His eyes duelled with hers, implacable, cold as the blue fire in the heart of a diamond.

'For a holiday.'

He didn't like that. The savage pressure increased until panic flared in her expression again. 'The truth, you little bitch. It was to contact Stephanie, wasn't it?' His arm moved, just enough for her to be able to speak again.

She drew in a deep sobbing breath, for clearly he knew. She nodded, watching him through the flickering fringe of her lashes. Violence swept the strong face, banishing the austerity she had thought an integral part of the man. A primitive bloodlust suffused his expression, at first colouring his skin, then leaving it white beneath the tan.

Flinching, she thought for a panic-stricken moment that he was going to kill her. Like a small animal with only one chance to escape a predator, she waited with a tense body for the moment.

But he fought the fury, and subdued it; she thought the strength of his self-control was even more frightening than the feral power of his anger.

'Why?' he whispered. 'Why did you need to contact her?' And when she didn't answer, he spat, 'Tell me, damn you. I won't have any compunction in forcing the answer from you, using whatever methods I have to.'

Sheer panic held her silent, her tongue refusing to work. In the furious struggle the sheet had slipped so that she was naked beneath him. He read her expression easily enough because he swore again, and said icily, 'I wouldn't touch you if you were the only woman left in the world, you treacherous little bitch. There are other methods of persuading you to talk, damn you. What did you want with Stephanie?'

'She's my half-sister,' she croaked.

Whatever he had expected it was not that. For a long, agonising moment he didn't react, and when he did it was with total and complete disbelief. She could see it in his face, in the renewed black fury of his expression.

Terrified, she hurried on, 'We have the same mother. I was born a year before she married Stephanie's father; I was adopted. When I found out who my mother was I also found out that she had had another daughter after she'd married, and that when she and her husband died the baby had been adopted by relatives in England.' She swallowed harshly. 'It was easy enough to discover who they were; when I visited my mother's grave I got talking to the locals, and they all knew that Stephanie's father was your mother's brother.'

The primal bloodlust seemed to have ebbed a little; staring at him, so close that his eyes dazzled her, she thought that now they were blank, as though she had thrown him a completely new ball, one he hadn't taken into consideration at all.

Still very cautious, she ventured, 'I didn't know whether she knew she was adopted, so I couldn't write to her, and besides, I wanted to see—I . . .' Her voice trailed away.

In one jerky movement he got up. For what seemed ages he stood staring down at her as though he had never seen her before, then abruptly he turned and paced across the floor, his lean body vibrating with caged energy, his eyes fixed on to some inward vision. Across to the window he went, and back again. She groped for the sheet and dragged it across to cover herself, then lay very still, swallowing carefully, one hand on her maltreated throat.

At last he swung around. 'Why didn't you contact me?'

She bit her lip. 'When I knew who had taken her I was appalled. I didn't know whether you would want to know, and I had no idea of how to go about getting in touch with you. Have you any idea how hard it is to find out anything about you? I had access to all sorts of information in the library where I work, but even then I had to rely mostly on gossip columns. You do a good job of keeping a low profile. And—I was scared. I don't suppose you have any idea of how dauntingly rich and powerful you are.'

Her voice was a husky whisper, and she had to swallow again. It hurt, and she did it very carefully. He frowned, his expression dark and withdrawn, his eyes running indifferently over her small, taut figure.

'If you had written, the letter would have got to me.'

'And what if you had decided that it would be bad for Stephanie? You'd have made sure that I never got near her.'

'Yes, probably.'

Indignantly, she sat up, saying hoarsely, 'So I did the right thing in bypassing you. And, whatever mistakes I made, you had no right to treat me like this.'

'Of course I did.' He snarled at her, his mouth thin, a muscle flicking along his jaw. 'You stupid——'

'Don't you dare!' She flung herself off the bed and stalked across to him, regal in spite of the fact that the sheet trailed on the floor behind her. 'You've called me enough names, thank you. I am not stupid——'

'Naïve, then. So gullibly raw that it never occurred to you that I might be bloody suspicious of anyone who tries to pick an acquaintance?'

'Why?' Her scorn was magnificent. 'Because you think everyone you come in contact with wants something from you?'

His gaze sharpened. 'Oh, that is definitely the truth. And before you lift that straight little nose, admit that you wanted something too. You wanted a sister. And to get her, you were prepared to do things you didn't really want to do, like make a small amount of love with your sister's adopted brother.'

Her mouth dropped open, but before she could tell him he was wrong he was making his way across the room. 'Hey!' she yelled, her voice rasping on the word. But he was already through the door, closing it behind him with a determined clunk.

He said from the other side, 'I'll have to check you out, of course, and until I know for sure you'll stay here.'

Sheer fury hurled her at the door, her fists thumping against the wood in a futile frenzy. It only lasted a minute before she regained control, and, exhausted and furious, her throat closing, she sat down on the bed and gazed fixedly at her feet, her brain racing around in circles.

About an hour later, after she had showered and resumed the sheet, there was a knock at the door. She stared suspiciously at it, and was all ready to break out into another angry tirade when Ailu appeared, bearing a bundle.

'Your clothes, madam,' she said without a flicker of expression.

So stunned was Candace that she watched with open mouth as the woman went out. Then, hardly breathing in case it was a cruel joke, she tried the door. It swung open. For a moment she dithered, fighting the impulse to flee just as she was. It took a massive dose of common sense to get herself into her clothes, and even then she dressed with the door partly open. After the few seconds needed to yank on a sundress and sandals she flew across to the doorway, her heart thumping heavily in her ears.

It gave on to a narrow passage, which led through a heavy door to a wider one that bisected the house. She hesitated, because there was no sound, no intimation of the presence of anyone else. Determination and a prickly defiance straightened her shoulders. Silently she walked to the wide double front doors and twisted the handle.

It didn't budge. Frustration clamped her teeth on to her bottom lip. She stood a moment staring at the coloured glass panels in the door, wondering viciously what Saul would say if she picked up the superb bronze art deco sculpture on the hall table and smashed it through the glass.

A lot, and none of it kind, she thought flippantly, reining in her temper. If she wanted to have any contact with Stephanie at all it would probably be a good idea to behave in a civilised manner. Besides, there were sensor beams placed carefully to cover the door and the windows.

However, no one could possibly object if she did a little exploring. With lips tightly folded she went into the first door on the left.

It was a plantation house, built probably at the end of the last century, so the rooms had high ceilings and great windows leading on to verandas shuttered against the fierce heat of the sun. The rooms that weren't locked, and presumably the three that were, were exquisitely furnished in a mixture of Victorian and modern furniture; there were flowers in all of the rooms, the hardwood floors were polished to gleaming splendour, and every window, every door on to the veranda, had locked screens over it.

She was, in fact, just as much a prisoner as she had been in what must have been the servant's bedroom. And Ailu, a massive presence in the kitchen, was still her warder. She answered Candace's questions with monosyllables that gave nothing away; some, she didn't answer at all.

Seething rage made Candace tremble, but she kept it under control, even managing to eat the dinner that Ailu prepared for her. Her throat was much better. Saul had known just how much pressure to apply for maximum effect with the least damage. Some effects of the sedative must have lingered, for after the meal she found herself yawning, her lids falling heavily over tired eyes. Nothing would persuade her back to the room that had been her prison, and she was still arguing with herself about what to do when she drifted off on the sofa in the drawing-room.

So she was at a complete disadvantage when Saul walked into the room, her eyes sultry with sleep, her hair rioting around her small flushed face as she tried to work out where she was. She even smiled at him as she pulled her skirt down past her knees, totally unaware that the bodice of the sunfrock had slid sideways.

He stopped as though she had shot him, his eyes blazing fiercely while they swept her face and then fell to her throat. Bewildered, she looked down, and saw a pink-tipped breast. Colour surged up through her skin; she shivered at the uncomfortable sensation of her nipple peaking and hauled the material up to cover herself, snapping, 'Voyeur!'

'Voyeurs,' he pointed out gently, 'go looking for sights. You were waiting for me.'

'I was not. I was asleep.'

He came into the room, his face sardonic, his eyes carefully veiled so that she couldn't see into them. 'It doesn't matter, anyway. I came to tell you that your explanation for your arrival here checked out.'

'Thank you,' she said with saccharine emphasis. 'You can't *know* how relieved I am to hear that.'

'So now,' he went on, ignoring her, 'we have to decide what to do with you.'

Her eyes narrowed. 'Do you?' she murmured dulcetly. 'I'll tell you what you do with me. First of all you let me go. And then you start apologising.'

She didn't like his smile, or the way his eyes swept the length of her body. And especially she didn't like the tone of his voice as he said, 'Any apologies, Candace, should come from you. I've been put to an enormous amount of trouble, I have had the security staff of the organisation running around in circles, I've had to put myself in jeopardy of various crimes, all because you didn't do the sensible thing and tell me why you wanted to meet Stephanie.'

'You've got a damned nerve.' She shot to her feet, staring around at the beautiful, serene room. 'Look, can we go outside? I feel smothered in here.'

He nodded. 'All right.'

Outside, the sudden tropical darkness had fallen, and the moon was once more high in the sky. Eagerly she stood on the veranda, taking deep breaths of the cool air, staring around her. They were still in the hills, for she could see far below to the lagoon where the light-fishers moved like small earthbound stars.

Candace shivered, demanding angrily, 'Why? That's all I want to know. Why did you have to kidnap me, bring me here, terrify the life out of me?'

'Because we didn't know what the hell you were up to,' he said.

'But you didn't even ask me! Why not? What gave you the idea that I was not just any ordinary tourist?'

He paused. 'A gut feeling,' he said slowly. 'Both Gil and I felt it. You seemed to—to be vibrating with some fierce emotion. And it was obvious that you had faked the faint at that first meeting—you didn't lose colour at all. Both Gil and I noticed that your attention was almost entirely focused on Stephanie, which made us even more suspicious.'

'Why?'

He showed his teeth. 'Because most women who try to pick an acquaintance have me firmly set in their sights.'

He waited for her to speak, but when she said nothing he went on, 'When you turned up at the house with a totally transparent story, I began to get more than a little worried. I got security to run a check on you and sent Lydia home and Stephanie to a more secure place and took you out to keep you busy, with Gil as a bloody chaperon watching every step you took just in case it was me you were after, either for money, or as part of some terrorist scheme.'

'I wondered,' she said involuntarily. 'You seem the sort of man who is well able to look after himself— I mean——'

'I know exactly what you mean, and normally I don't have bodyguards dogging my private life. So, you and I and Gil spent as much time as possible together while details of your file began to build up. It was interesting.

A childhood characterised by an unusual amount of rejection, turbulent years at high school, clever enough to
win a scholarship to university, a rebellious two years
there, then you dropped out and spent a year away from
New Zealand, no one knew where. A year you were
bloody evasive about when I asked you what you'd
done.'

She stared at him. 'What's that got to do with
anything?'

'It was a year when you couldn't be traced. You could
have spent it at a camp learning the devil-damned skills
terrorists need.'

She said stonily, 'I went youth-hostelling around
Europe and Great Britain.'

His mouth twisted, but his voice was smooth and cold
and deadly serious. 'And then, of course, there was the
fact that word had filtered through that there was likely
to be an attempt on Stephanie. We didn't know whether
it was just a baseless whisper, or whether there were a
few cold hard facts to back it up, and until we found
out we were not going to relax our vigilance.'

Colour drained from her face. She asked jerkily, 'What
do you mean, an attempt?'

'Kidnapping.' The word hung ugly and heavy on the
humid air. 'It happens, Candace. Do you know how my
parents died?'

She nodded. 'In a plane accident.'

'That was what we wanted the world to think. They
were kidnapped by a terrorist organisation which wanted
a large amount of money. Worse than that, they wanted
Jerrard's to pull out of a government deal, and that
would have destabilised a South American country
enough to make it ripe for a takeover.'

She was white now, her eyes enormous in her face.
His level voice and composed face were more frightening than any display of emotion could have been. She
said huskily, 'What happened?'

'I don't think you want to know. They died. But every one of the terrorists died too, thanks to some brilliant, dedicated work by the security branch of Jerrard's, helped by government departments from several countries. After that débâcle it's not likely that anyone would try the same thing again, but there are always fanatics who believe that they will be the ones able to pull it off the next time. If I were snatched, Jerrard's would be under the management of a board who collectively are as hard-nosed as I am. They would let me die rather than jeopardise the organisation. But if Stephanie were taken—I think I would do what I was told, to keep her alive.'

She was cold, icy tremors racking her body. Shaking her head, she whispered, 'But—surely—you didn't believe that I would—I could——?'

'Thanks to the fact that you hadn't told us anything, we didn't know what the hell you were up to,' he returned savagely. 'And if you were a terrorist or a kidnapper I didn't want to alert you before we had found out who you were working with. After discussions with security I decided that the best thing to do was keep you out of harm's way until we had more information. Which explains the somewhat melodramatic way I brought you here, and the reason you were sedated. I didn't want you contacting anyone.'

She had to concentrate on what he was saying, put everything else out of her mind so that by the time she could allow herself to feel emotion again she would be better equipped to deal with the pain.

'So you were suspicious right from the start,' she said in a remote little voice. 'I wondered.'

'When we realised that you had deliberately engineered that first meeting, we were suspicious enough to keep an eye on you, but it wasn't until you sailed to the house that we were convinced you were up to something, especially as we knew that you had been on the tourist trip and been warned not to land on the beach. There was someone watching you on the boat.'

He watched her painful blush with a cool, dispassionate glance, possibly waiting for her to say something. Shame held her silent, and he resumed, 'But we still didn't know whether you were part of a scheme to get to Stephanie, or merely using her as a lever to get to me.'

'You've got a——'

'I've got power and money,' he said calmly, matter-of-factly, 'the greatest aphrodisiacs in the world. A large bank balance does a lot for anyone's sex life. Of course, that was the simplest explanation, but somehow it didn't ring true, and a little closer acquaintance with you proved that it was definitely Stephanie you were interested in, not me. You asked after her, and were disappointed when she wasn't about, and I was able to get you to go with me simply by suggesting that we'd be seeing her.'

'I'd have been a very inept terrorist,' she snapped, furious to think that she had given herself away so easily.

'Possibly, but you could have been a tool, someone dispensable, a fool carried away by the romance of terrorism.' His intonation was icy with contempt. 'As for the other possibility, when I tested you with a few kisses, it was clearly not what you had in mind. Oh, you endured them——'

'Don't be an idiot,' she said gruffly.

He showed his teeth in a smile. 'I didn't get where I am today by running away from the truth. You were attracted, but there was a definite holding back. So that left us with another, infinitely more unpleasant possibility. You had to be part of the nebulous plot to take Stephanie. Probably not here. It would be almost impossible for anyone to manage a kidnapping and not have half the island aware of it. There are eyes everywhere on Fala'isi.'

'You managed it,' she said curtly.

'Because I'm an islander. No, we surmised that probably you only wanted to make contact here, form a bond, a basis of friendship, so that she'd trust you when you got in touch with her later; the actual snatch would take place somewhere where the odds were more in your favour. That established, I took steps to keep you occupied, while others searched your luggage and watched Stephanie. You were right about that, incidentally. The man who searched your room didn't realise he'd been careless. He'll know better the next time.'

Pain splintered through her body. She drew in a jagged breath, but kept upright, her eyes fixed on the angular mask of his features.

'But we found nothing,' he continued, still in that same calm, reasonable tone. 'We needed more time and the easiest way to buy it was to put you out of circulation for a while. So you ended up here. The locals think you and I are enjoying an affair. No one was suspicious— why should they be? I made sure that plenty of people saw us together. By the time we got back after our day on the boat everyone assumed that I had found someone to take Lydia's place.'

'So you had it all worked out.' There, her voice could stay flat and emotionless too.

'I love Stephanie.' He shrugged. 'I would do anything and everything that's necessary to keep her safe.'

Well, Candace could understand that. Her hand went to her throat. She was even paler than a moment ago, but when she realised what she was doing she let her hand drop to her side and her chin came up.

His wide shoulders sketched a shrug. 'We've spent this afternoon checking your story. Fortunately for you, it's true.'

Her senses had been sharpened on some emotional whetstone. She could see the way the moonlight highlighted the bold lines of his face, and her skin prickled with his nearness, her nostrils flaring slightly at his scent, indefinably male with the faintest hint of aftershave. Stronger than that were the tropical perfumes of the flowers, frangipani and the little native gardenia.

She should hate him, but Candace felt as though she had just stepped over a precipice, dropped through space and time to another plane, another dimension, another period of existence. Later, she would realise that that was when she fell in love with him, as opposed to being blindly and violently attracted to him.

But at the moment she had other things to consider. 'The threat to Stephanie,' she said urgently. 'The rumour, or whisper, or whatever it was. Does that still stand? Is she still in danger?'

'We've found the source of that, too.' His voice was almost abstracted, but she shuddered. 'A disaffected employee, one who was sacked and tried to regain a little of his lost prestige by making wild threats and insinuations in bars. Normally we wouldn't have taken much notice of him, but he boasted that he had had contacts with radical groups. He's no longer an issue.'

'What happened to him?'

Something glittered in his gaze. 'He's been warned, and, as he's sensible enough when he's sober, that's an end to it.' Mockery tinged his tone. 'Why, did you think I'd had him killed?'

She held his gaze. 'You had the terrorists who murdered your parents killed, didn't you?'

He said nothing, but his very silence was an answer of sorts.

Shivering, she moved away, down from the veranda on to a path that led through thick growth to a tiny stream. It flowed quietly at their feet, but a few yards further on it began to chatter over stones in a little waterfall. Almost immediately she had to stop, for she had arrived at the edge of a stretch of water, still and shiny, a sheet of obsidian beneath the paler sky. From it a thin spire of water, silver as the moon, evanescent

as mist, stretched up into the sky, seemingly motionless
until the soft hiss of water falling into water below revealed that it arrived back into the pool almost as at-
tenuated as gossamer.

'It's beautiful,' she whispered, stopping. 'Why is it
here?'

His voice came from just behind her. 'One of the
Chapman ancestors had this made for his mistress. She
lived in the cottage.'

'It's terribly romantic, but why didn't she live at the
house?'

He shrugged. 'His wife and family were in the house.'

'Oh.'

She saw his teeth flash. 'You don't approve?'

'No,' she said slowly. 'No, I don't. I think promises
are made to be kept.'

'Yes. They all seemed to live happily enough. Keep
going, this path takes us back to the cottage.'

The narrow path, wide enough only for two, wound
past another, smaller pool. In it there were water-lilies,
their folded white buds pointing to the sky, each in a
nest of round leaves amid spirals of water that indicated
goldfish. It was very still, very calm, a Monet in blacks
and silvers. Around it the garden, scented and breath-
takingly beautiful in the moonlight, swirled in to form
a frame for the fountain out on the lake. Blotting out
the stars, a jagged outline denoted one of the mountains
thrown up from the heart of the earth far below in an
unimaginable cataclysm.

Candace shivered again. He had not answered her
question, and for some reason the answer was of vital
importance to her. But she waited until they were back
on the veranda before she asked him again. This time
he did give her an answer, of sorts.

'They died resisting arrest,' he said remotely.

She pushed a little harder. 'But it was you who——'

Too hard. He rounded on her, his face drawn and pale and icily, savagely predatory. 'They had killed my mother—even now I can't——'

'I'm sorry.' She must have run across to him, because she took him in her arms, holding him with all her strength, saying remorsefully, 'I shouldn't have pushed, I'm sorry, Saul...'

His arms came around her in a bone-crushing embrace; as if unused to such open sympathy, he stared into her eyes, his own for once revealing a torment that brought tears to hers.

She lifted a hand and curved it around his cheek. 'It's over,' she said soberly. 'But I understand why you believed you had to take no chances. It's all right. I'm sorry I brought it all back.'

He moved abruptly, wrapping her even closer, his cheek pressed against the warm silk of her hair.

She stood very still, looking across the still silence of water-lilies and water to where the fountain hissed. A vagrant breeze caught at it and water fell like a veil across the column. She caught her breath, for it seemed to her that she saw a white rainbow, insubstantial as a dream, form in the spray. She felt his head turn, his eyes follow hers.

'A moonbow,' he said on a note of wonder, as shaken as she was by the beautiful thing. 'I've never seen one before.'

The breeze died, the veil of water fell silently into the pool, and the moonbow was gone.

She felt tears well up in her eyes and said in a soft, husky little voice, 'That was beautiful, so beautiful... Thank you for bringing me here.'

He looked down into her enraptured face, then his arms loosened slightly around her and the enchantment of the moment, airy, insubstantial and moonlit, was transmuted into something just as magical but infinitely more basic, rooted not in faerie but in the earth, the primitive throb of hunger that called woman to man, man to woman.

His mouth fastened on hers with a starving need, taking all that she had to give, all her strength, all her generous spirit, all her sweet surrender.

The emotion of the past few minutes must have knocked her off balance, for in spite of everything she responded with ardour and enthusiasm. As she would always do, she realised with a lurch of the heart that owed nothing to his desperate passion. Because she loved him.

The real thing, Romeo and Juliet stuff. 'O, she doth teach the torches to burn bright!'

She had been right to be terrified of this. Even as his mouth sought hers again she knew that this was what she had feared all of her life—not passion, not even love, but her own response to it. Since the age of ten, when she had understood that she was alone, she had guarded her heart because she had somehow understood that she was capable of this overwhelming subjugation of her senses that swamped the cool logic of her brain, common sense and intelligence—all lost in the honeyed mixture of fire and sweetness that was coursing through her veins now.

'And you are beautiful.' He had a deep voice, exciting, many-layered with tone and meaning, and she shuddered to hear it.

She was shaken, exalted, by the gentleness of that kiss. It was unlike the others she had had from him, almost tentative, seducingly sweet. Relaxing, she let that enchanter's wizardry flow over her, her bones melting at the further touch of his mouth. Her arms came up, her hands touched the proud dark head, sliding through the crisp thickness of his hair to hold him close as he bent again to her.

He lifted his mouth and said her name in a shaken voice, softly, and then he kissed her once more, only this time it was with the hard, hot fierceness of need, his hunger calling to hers, both joining in a conflagration that almost overwhelmed them, so that when he lifted his mouth to breathe she was making soft, muffled little sounds in her throat and the eyes that were revealed by the slow rise of her lashes were glazed and dark as the pool in the pallor of her face.

Her tongue came out to touch her lips, then retreated when his crystalline gaze fastened on to it. The heated stain across his arrogant cheekbones, the pulse throbbing at his temple, gave credence to an atavistic intuition that told her that now was the time to say no and call a halt before it was too late.

If she drew back now he would accept her decision, and she would never know what it was like to make love with him. Her lashes drooped; she leaned her head on his chest, thankful that he was letting her make the decision by herself.

From the time she had realised that not only her father but her mother had betrayed her, her whole life had been founded on caution. She had never let herself be lured into a position where more pain could be inflicted on her. Now, as though she had been blind all her life and could suddenly see, she realised how limiting her wariness had been. Along with pain and disillusion she had cut out of her life joy and eagerness and desire. Now, in his arms, in this magic place, an untapped recklessness ran like an energy flow through her body.

His head came down. He bit her ear very gently, and his warm breath played about the sensitive whorls and curlicues, setting off a million small shocks right through her system.

She gasped, and his chest lifted as he laughed beneath his breath. Indistinctly she realised that he too was in thrall to this unknown passion, and, made bold by newly liberated instincts, she stood on her toes and touched the tip of her tongue to the hollow at the base of the brown column of his throat.

His chest rose and fell again sharply, but this time there was no amusement in his voice as he asked, 'Do you know what you're doing?'

'Yes.' The word feathered across the damp skin where her tongue had touched him.

He said grimly, 'I hope so,' and tangled his hands in the soft waves of her hair as he pulled her head back gently for his kiss.

'Ailu,' she whispered with her last remnant of common sense.

'She went home.'

What followed was as natural as the moon and the subdued song of the fountain. The mysterious silver light played about them as they kissed, and soon, inevitably, kissing was not enough. His mouth touched the pulse that throbbed in her throat, and the fragile slope of her shoulder. He must have heard her indrawn breath, but he could not know that to her untutored body his touch was wine and dark magic and smooth, sweet fire. She had no thought of saying no, no desire to rein back the fierce thrill of response that ran like forked lightning through her veins.

His hands were sure, gentle yet unrelenting as they touched her shoulders, the soft skin of her arms, and at last the curve of her breast. She shivered, and he laughed beneath his breath.

'Do you like that? Tell me what you like, Candace, and I'll give it to you. Anything—anything you want, I can give you.'

She couldn't speak. The words stumbled and dried in her mouth as she looked up into eyes that blazed into hers, burning away inhibitions and fear until she was left at the mercy of her long-repressed hunger.

'Do you like this?' His hand skimmed over the point of her breast, barely touching it, yet she felt a strange drawing sensation there, and a heaviness that seemed to weigh down her bones and her limbs.

'Or this?' He bent and his mouth touched the ultra-sensitive nub, hot and moist through the fine material.

She cried out aloud, and he smiled without humour, and said, 'Yes, I see you do.'

The world turned dizzily. She barely had time to realise that he was picking her up when he set her down again on the cushions of the biggest lounger.

He stripped off his shirt and dropped it carelessly to the floor, then came down beside her. For moment the old atavistic fear of a woman for a predatory male rose in her; she didn't flinch away, but her muscles tensed.

His face devoid of expression, starkly austere, he said quietly, 'You have only to say no. I'm no rapist,' and she realised how stupid she was being.

'I'm sorry,' she said, adding half beneath her breath, 'I should be used to being small. And you,' with a shy smile, 'suddenly seemed very big.'

Indeed, his lean elegance was deceptive. She stared, fascinated, at shoulders wide enough to block out the moon, arms and chest corded with muscles that moved with potent power beneath sleek bronzed skin.

'I suppose life can sometimes be frightening for a woman as small as you are,' he said, but his voice was detached, and he was toying with a curl at her temple, pulling at the warm tress with a sure, gentle touch as though he loved the feel of the silk over his skin.

She said, 'I feel safe with you,' and was startled by the sudden keen flash of intelligence in his eyes. Then they narrowed and he bent and kissed her throat.

'Safety is not exactly what I have in mind,' he said against the soft skin. 'In fact, I think you may well be one of the most dangerous women I have ever met.' He paused, then continued, 'And I feel far from brotherly.'

She touched his head, felt an arm slide behind her as his mouth pressed her back into the cushions. Her head slid back, baring her throat to his avid, open-mouthed kisses, and she gave a tiny sigh. Common sense was drowned in a flood of rightness, as though she had spent all her life waiting for this, for this man. No stranger, but the other half of her...

The moonlight moved across the floor of the terrace, first revealing the slow, silent progress of their love-making, but then, when he slid the sundress from her body, the tactful moon moved on and left them in darkness. Lost in the sensual haze created by his hands and mouth, Candace watched voluptuously as his dark head bent over her breasts, moving so lightly, so softly, that she gave a muffled cry of protest and longing.

The muscles across the back of his neck flexed as he continued tormenting her with the heated touch of his mouth. It was almost painful, her breasts jutting as they begged for his mouth, while the rest of her untrained body was liquid, flowing, melting, aching with a savage need.

'Saul, please.' It should have been a command, but there was a pleading note in her voice that frightened her, because there was nothing she could do about it.

His breath came hot on her dampened nipple as he laughed.

'Please what?'

'Please—help me.'

He held still for a moment, as though her words had surprised him, but when her hips moved in an instinctive little movement against his leg he lowered his head, and drew the throbbing aureole into the heated cavern of his mouth.

Candace gave a choked cry, her whole body stiffening as a wave of sensation poured over her, taking her with it to some region where she was lost, her only hope of salvation the man who was suckling her with such magician's sensuality.

Her hands clenched, then relaxed, and she surrendered, offering him the slender length of her body, all the fire and passion she had kept behind bars until then. Her ledger of pain and pleasure was closed, tossed away into oblivion.

She was about to receive some sort of revelation, be initiated into a mystery as old as time, as young as tomorrow, and her whole being rejoiced that it was this man, this night, this moon, that had joined to make her come alive for the first time.

the ... coulda too relaxed, at length real-
... y, trying, and the noble taught to her cool...
them and ... since the ... begun I should assume year...
... home of gathered, between it fresh, tough, teem...
... so much ...

# CHAPTER SEVEN

SAUL lifted his head, and Candace was bereft, cold, for-saken, until he said, 'Touch me, Candace. Don't make me do all the work.'

The words hurt in some obscure fashion, but she was too far gone to analyse the reason. His eyes weren't cold now. Even in the friendly darkness she could see that they were molten, a blue hot enough to burn in, inciting her to do things she had only ever read about, miracu-lously freeing her from shame or inhibitions. Wonder-ingly, her small hands traced the scroll of hair on his chest, realising with something close to incredulity that he stiffened under her touch. She smiled, a blind little movement of lips slightly swollen by his deep kisses, and leaned forward to see if his nipples were as sensitive as hers, if they begged for the heat of her mouth.

Her tongue curled around the little nub, retreated, then ventured forth again. He said something, the sound rumbling in his chest, and she laughed, and touched the other one, lightly, as delicately as a butterfly settling on a flower.

He shuddered, and she yielded to the dark and dangerous tides at play in her and bit the nipple gently, before soothing it with her mouth. Her hands roved across his chest, felt the rigid stillness of the muscles there, moved down to his ribs, and discovered the lean tautness of his midriff and waist.

At the waistband of his trousers she stopped, and looked up at him. He was watching her, his face all angles, fierce and boldly jutting, stripped of everything but a hunger so untamed that those first tendrils of fear came back with a rush. She could see a bead of sweat on his brow, and was amazed at the savage pagan pleasure that flooded through her, replacing the fear.

'Yes,' he said harshly. 'You like seeing me like this, don't you? Let's see if I can return the compliment.'

He twisted, forcing her over his arm, and took her breast in his mouth, drawing on it almost to the point of pain, until she moaned. His head lifted; he looked into her rapturous face, and the beautiful line of his mouth moved in a smile that was as forbidding as it was stark and full of promise.

'I can't bear it,' she whispered, closing her eyes to shut out the sight of his face, almost unmoved yet so strangely intense.

'I know. It's beyond endurance, yet we can't bear not to experience it.'

He settled her back against the cushions and stood up to haul off the rest of his clothes, revealing himself in full masculine arousal. Her mouth dry, Candace stared at him, watching with fascinated pleasure as the muscles in his lean legs and back flexed in wonderful symmetry beneath the warm, oiled silk of his skin.

She was no longer afraid. Her body was singing with frustration and the knowledge that soon it would be assuaged, and she lifted herself up to remove her sandals.

'Let me,' he said in a thick voice.

His fingers on her were a torment, his mouth, as it followed the slow, erotic progress of his hands up her legs, at once a punishment and the rarest of pleasures. She felt her muscles stiffening, and tried hard to control them, but her body began to move in sinuous little shudders, her hips pushing, asking, pleading.

At the fork of her body the fire he had built so carefully blazed out of control; she looked at him in all his dark pagan glory and her eyes dilated endlessly, without volition, wordlessly calling him to the blazing conflagration that would send them both to unknown realms of satiation.

For a charged moment he stared down into her enraptured face, his own carved in stone like some old, brutal god intent only on victory and pillage, and then he gave a deep, shuddering sigh and as if beyond control he moved over her and she knew at last the fierce rapture of unity, the primitive melding of bodies, the irresistible masculine force that invaded and conquered, yet was in turn conquered by her softer female strength.

At the first fierce thrust of his body she cried out, the words floating unheard through the heated shimmering air, but there was no pain and little discomfort, merely a kind of rearrangement, as though her body was accustoming itself to something long awaited and eagerly anticipated.

Then she forgot to be surprised at how simple it was, and gave herself up to the kind of primitive claiming, a taking and giving so powerful, so bewilderingly ecstatic that she was wrenched from the foundations of her past and sent spinning into another world where sensation ruled.

He wrapped her in a cloak of fire and light, the exquisite sensation of skin against skin, silk sliding erotically over silk, the heat of his body, its weight and the tensile strength of muscles and sinews. She was lost in the fragrance of their love, a mixture of the clean masculine perfume that was his and the scent of her own femininity, blending to form an essence so arousing that the gardenias faded into dimness against it.

But most of all she was conscious of the overwhelming possession, the male dominance, the female envelopment, so right at this moment; the way her body accepted his joyously, fearlessly, and made its own claims, secure in the knowledge that they would be met.

But tension began to overtake the pleasure that held her in thrall; restlessly she started to twist in fiery little movements that sought something else, something more, something beyond the tide of passion she was drowning in.

He said sharply, 'Don't do that! I can't——'

But she arched up, and as if a dam had burst his response shuddered through her, catching her up, carrying her away. Every cell in her body was drenched in sweetness, seared by flames. Terrified, she fought against the tide, but it caught her up and vanquished her, submerging her in sensations so intense that she thought she fainted.

The taut strength of his body collapsed; he was suddenly a heavy weight, the heated slickness of his skin sliding across her as he moved to the side of the lounger. Above the thunder of her heart she could hear the deep rasp of his breath mingled with the heavy sound of hers. She felt exhausted, her body limp and slack, yet elated and so light that she thought she might float off the cushions and across the terrace, rise as lightly and silently as the fountain and mingle with the foam and the night and the moonbow.

Slowly her heart-rate eased down to something like its normal speed. The air flowed humid and scented across her skin, but she became conscious of a chill that owed nothing to the atmosphere, because it was caused by the man who lay beside her on the lounger, as close as a whisper, as far away as the impersonal stars.

Her teeth worried her lip; she didn't know what to say or do. Surely he could not make love to her so—so voraciously!—then reject her, yet it was rejection she felt coming towards her in waves. Suddenly it all became sordid, their bodies sprawled in voluptuous abandon, the passion that had seemed for a short while to transcend the physical now revealed for the brutal animal thing that it really was.

Shame and humiliation swept over her. Shivering, she began to sit up.

'Lie still,' he commanded softly. He turned and pulled her against him. 'Are you cold?'

'No.'

'Lonely?' He gave a soft laugh as she melted into him. 'I'm sorry. I am not used to such—a cataclysmic reaction. I was wondering whether I've just made a bigger fool of myself than ever before.'

'You?' She lifted her head to look at him, her eyes betrayingly astonished.

'Yes, me.' His mouth twisted in wry amusement. 'In spite of your not very flattering opinion of me, I'm not promiscuous.' She said nothing, but he smiled, not particularly pleasantly. 'I don't sleep with every woman I take out, or every one who spends the holidays at my house. I have always been able to control my appetites. Up until now.'

Hope leapt in her breast, irradiated her eyes. Did he mean Lydia? Of course such a statement had nothing to do with love, but she was so enamoured of him that she would take anything she could get. She gave him a smile that glowed with radiance. They were now in deep darkness, the moon hidden behind the overhang of the veranda directly overhead, but she saw his answering smile, and wondered at the lop-sided cynicism she thought she discerned.

'I'm not promiscuous either,' she said abruptly.

'Was that the first time?'

Suddenly shy, she nodded, watching from between lowered lashes to see how he would take this.

He lay very still, then slid his hands into the thick mass of her hair and pulled her head up so that he could kiss her. His mouth on hers was soft and slow and determined, and incredibly she could feel her sated body begin to stir, the flow of sensation pick up through her veins.

She gave a little gasp, and he laughed, a sensuous sound that echoed in her ears for days afterwards.

'Amazing, isn't it?' he murmured. 'For me it should be impossible, and for little virgins it should be almost so.'

Magnificent in his nudity, he stood up and held out a commanding hand. 'Come with me,' he said.

Without any hesitation she put her hand in his and followed him into the darkness of the house until he unlocked a door and switched on a light.

She made a gasping expression of astonishment, for they were standing in a room made for love, from the explicit and exquisite painting of two embracing lovers above the enormous divan, to the satin coverings and pillows that scattered its head and the erotic textures of fur in the enormous rugs on the floor.

'The man who had this decorated didn't know the meaning of restraint,' Saul said, smiling into Candace's dazzled eyes as she took it all in, 'so it seems appropriate that we make love in here too. I don't feel like an intruder, do you? Perhaps the room misses being a haven for lovers.'

She couldn't drag her eyes away from his to stare around at the incredible room, but some musky savour, perhaps a lingering trace of the scent worn by the woman who had once pleasured her lover there, made her skin go tight with anticipation. She said huskily, 'No, I don't feel like an intruder. In fact, there's nowhere else I'd rather be.'

He lifted her lightly, easily, and carried her across to the wide divan, setting her down on the smooth cool silk with deliberation.

Something reckless gleamed in the brilliant depths of his eyes, something she responded to even as she mistrusted it. 'Then let's take it slow and gentle this time,' he said as he came down beside her, 'and we'll love as if it's the last time, the only time we ever have together.'

A *frisson* of foreboding touched her lightly. Something was wrong, devastatingly so. Her brows drew together, but he bent and kissed the small hollow of her

navel, and as she felt his tongue touch her skin a slither
of sensation rendered everything in her mind lost and
forgotten.

He had said he was not promiscuous. She believed
him; he was too fastidious for self-indulgence. But he
had made love to enough women to know exactly how
to wring the last ounce of pleasure from her, expertly
using his skill and sensitivity to show her the many ways
a man and a woman could complement each other in
love. Blindly, she followed where he led, whispering
words she would never have dreamed she could say,
touching him with innocent carnality, worshipping his
sleek masculine strength in every way that came to her
mind. She learned the myriad flavours and textures of
his body, gloried in the contrast between the pale ivory
of her skin and the darker tones of his, the soft curves
of her body and his long, powerful muscles.

He made love with a potent confidence that she found
intoxicating, his expression absorbed as he took her with
him into a realm that encompassed only that bed, a
kingdom where both reigned supreme.

She did not care that she had no control over her body,
that her will was lost in a haze of passion, because she
had only to look into the drawn strength of his face,
meet the blazing invitation of his eyes, to know that he
too was lost in their lovemaking, as intent and absorbed
by the feel of her in his arms, against his mouth, as she
was by him.

Finally, with a gasping entreaty, he guided her on to
him, lying back against the cushions like a pasha of old,
arrogantly sure of his victory. She resisted, but only for
a moment, then submitted, holding her body proudly as
she eased down over him.

'I can see you properly like this,' he said, his voice
almost guttural, his eyes widened into darkness as they
scanned her slender, flushed body, the satin curves of

her breasts, high and proud, the peaks tipped and hard from the fierce ministrations of his mouth.

Colour flooded her skin, and he laughed deep in his throat and put out a lazy hand to touch her breast, letting it lie there with open possession before he trailed it down to the narrow indentation of her waist. His fingers bit in as she settled down, encompassing him, enfolding him, taking him deep inside her. Sensation sprang like an arrow through her, making her gasp and begin to move helplessly, setting the pace, the tell-tale colour spreading from her breasts to her face as slowly, sensuously, they found the rhythm that suited them both.

It was different, yet in some ways even more satisfying than that first tumultuous time. But the resolution in both instances was inevitable, a violent concatenation that hurled them into ecstasy and exhaustion and satisfaction too intense to be borne.

She went to sleep with him beside her, and slept so heavily that she heard nothing, felt nothing.

When she woke it was not yet dawn, but she was alone on the divan. At first she lay, waiting for him to come back, but after several minutes she pushed her hands across to the other side of the bed and discovered that it was cool, as though he had left as soon as she had fallen asleep.

She got up and went into the bathroom, switching the light on. For a moment she stood stunned, blinking rapidly as she looked around the incredible room. It had been decorated to look like a grotto, with a waterfall down one wall and a pool of black marble set in rocks and boulders. Orchids, white and cream and green, grew with lush foliage plants and ferns among the rocks. In that bath a naked woman would look like a houri, white-skinned and pampered, there only for her master's pleasure.

Candace swallowed and closed her eyes briefly, then hooked a bathsheet from the rail and went out, turning off the light. She wrapped herself in the soft towelling as she walked across to the window. With cold hands she turned the handle on the screen and pushed it wide.

The fountain soared upwards, a fine thin line in the grey pre-dawn light, falling with a muted hiss into the black pool. From out of the depths of the trees came the liquid notes of a bird, mockingly, like an echo of love betrayed... The fabled, rarely seen bird that was supposed to summon a lover for whoever had heard it.

And not just any old lover; no, the bird summoned the one love, the ultimate soul mate...

A stark little smile hurt her mouth. Well, it had called her lover to her, but, in the way of so many of the myths, it cheated even while it delivered what it had promised. Saul had been all that a woman could ask for, fierce and tender, passionate and honest. In his arms, in his bed, she had found rapture beyond the normal dimension and a release that had astounded and frightened her. She had discovered herself to be as innately sensual as he.

The fountain played steadily, softly, into the black smooth depths of the pool, a maddening, monotonous background to the thoughts that kept whirring crazily around her head.

When the swift tropical dawn finally broke in its glory of pink and gold over the island she was still standing at the window, watching the way the light tinted the fountain. To the man who walked softly up the path from the pool she looked like a wraith.

She didn't turn when he came into the lovely, sensual room, or give any sign of noticing his arrival. It wasn't until he came across to stand beside her that she looked up at him with great empty eyes. He was dressed in the clothes he had worn the night before, a dark shirt, darker trousers, but he had half rolled the sleeves up, and in the dim morning light he looked tough and intimidating.

He asked curtly, 'All right, how much do you want?'

She said nothing, but her lashes quivered and fell, and she turned away from him sullied and defiled by his cynicism.

'How much?' he persisted. 'Virginity is quite a selling point among some men. I've never bothered about it before but I'm prepared to recompense you for the loss of your maidenhead. And you were enchantingly and very seductively wanton. I've seldom enjoyed a night more.'

The muscles in her throat worked but her voice was thick with pain and she could only say his name.

'Or did you come here looking for even bigger game? Do you think that being Stephanie's illegitimate half-sister entitles you to live off her?'

Her gaze flashed up. He was smiling, the predatory hawk's features set in an expression that iced her heart. Her hand came up to hide her face as she whispered, 'No. Oh, no! How could you...?'

He was going to say something more but she made an abrupt gesture, and, swallowing, went on in a clear, toneless voice, 'I came to Fala'isi to see her. That was all. When I realised that I might be able to meet her I—I couldn't resist. I wasn't going to tell her who I was. I didn't even know whether she was aware that she'd been adopted. I wouldn't have told her. But I did want to see her.' She looked pleadingly at him. 'You must understand, Saul. As far as I know she's my only living relative.'

'Your natural father?'

Her mouth tightened. 'He fled to Australia when he found out that my mother was pregnant. He was a boy who had come from Europe after the war—no one seemed to know what nationality he was, but when he arrived here they gave him the surname Smith. I tried, but I couldn't find him.'

'And of course even if you did, he wasn't likely to be as rich as Stephanie.'

Her mouth moved in a cold, pale smile. 'I can tell you until I'm blue in the face that I'm not interested in your damned money, but you're not going to believe me, are you? At least I didn't fool myself into thinking that you would be pleased to learn of an inconvenient half-sister lurking about.'

'Oh, you could prove it,' he said. He waited until she was looking at him with painful attention and then he said evenly, 'You could go away and never contact her again.'

She whitened. 'You don't know what you're asking.'

'A little compassion.' But there was no compassion in the words that crackled through the air, or in the cold inimical eyes that watched her so calmly. 'I can understand why you want to meet Stephanie, but even if I accept that you have no mercenary aims, look at it from her point of view. She's hardly likely to welcome a sister from the wrong side of the blanket, one who has nothing in common with her, nothing but an accident of birth.'

White to the lips, she whispered, 'How could you...?'

He turned away, hands shoved firmly into the pockets of his trousers. 'I think it will be better for everyone if you just fade out of her life, a tourist she met once. Forget that you've met her.'

'And last night's seduction?' she asked with aloof interest. 'Will I forget that as well?'

He sucked in a deep breath. 'It shouldn't have happened, but it was inevitable. We both realised that, didn't we, from the first time we set eyes on each other?'

'But it's not going to happen again.'

'No,' he agreed. 'It's not going to happen again. An affair—but you can see that, as things are, that's impossible.'

Was that a note of relief in the deep, imperturbable tones? Was he pleased that she was being 'reasonable'?

Because he was right. There could be no future for them, even if he had wanted one, which he manifestly did not. Stephanie had brought them together, but apart from Stephanie they had nothing in common except for an antagonistic, overwhelming desire. Which he had apparently slaked. And the fact that she was in love with him, which was a nuisance, but no concern of his.

'Very well,' she said coolly. 'I'll leave today.'

Frowning, he said, 'I'll recompense you for your holiday, and for frightening——'

Something snapped inside her. She rounded on him, her eyes blazing, and screamed, 'I don't want a penny of your tainted money. If it means so much to you, you need it far more than I do! I came to see my sister, not to live off her, not to sell myself to you! Whatever you got from me I gave freely and without counting the cost. I don't want anything from you—you couldn't give me enough to fill one corner of my heart. Just leave me alone!'

His head snapped back as though she had hit him. Beneath the golden tan his skin was pale and around his mouth there was a thin white line. For a moment his incredible eyes hooked her through the heart, and then, with an effort of will so concentrated as to be almost palpable, he subdued the savage emotions her tirade had called forth and said implacably, 'Very well. I'll have your clothes packed and waiting, and the Learjet is ready to take you to Auckland. However, before you go, I want this signed.'

It was a sheet of paper, the words scrawled over it in his slashing handwriting. They danced, black and forbidding before her eyes. Pain jagged through her body so that she seemed to shudder with it. She ripped the paper into two pieces and said contemptuously, 'I'm not going to promise never to contact Stephanie again. Not even you with all your power and your money could hold me to it if I did, but I'm not going to sign. One day she'll want to know more about her family. And when she does, I'll be waiting. Because she's my sister, and we have the right to know each other.'

His expression brought an icy thrill of fear down her spine but she stood her ground, holding her head high, meeting the stark threat in his face with a proud hauteur that was new to her, born out of pain and courage.

She thought she saw a reluctant respect in those deep eyes, but if it happened he hid it so quickly that she couldn't be sure. When he spoke it was to say something that astounded her. 'Promise me something, Candace.'

She stared, unable to believe her ears. 'What?'

'That you'll contact me if you ever need help.'

The muscles in her shoulders protested at being held so rigidly. She gave a cracked laugh. 'No, I don't need your help. I've always managed, I'll keep on managing.'

'Don't be so bloody stupid!'

Good, she had broken through the dark mask of control. But he subdued his emotions immediately, finishing in a voice stiff with anger, 'Don't try to contact Stephanie.'

She gave him a long, considering stare from those empty eyes. He looked the same as he had always looked, hard, emotionless, all of the fire and passion of the night before banished by an iron will.

'Is this the way you pay off all your mistresses? With a kick in the teeth?'

He said curtly, 'You are not my mistress.'

She produced a smile. 'No, merely a one-night stand.'

'Exactly.'

In a voice that began with a tremble but hardened immediately, she returned, 'Does Stephanie know she's adopted?'

He said after a long moment, 'That's not any business of yours, Candace.'

'No, of course not. However, from my own experience, it's better to find out sooner than later. And I give you fair warning that, in spite of everything you might do, I intend to contact her again when she's twenty.'

'And I give you fair warning that I'll do everything I can to prevent it. The car is waiting at front of the house. Your things are in it.'

She said slowly, 'How do you know I won't go to the newspapers with this?'

His broad shoulders moved in a shrug. 'You aren't the sort. You value your privacy too highly.'

She turned away. 'Thank you.' All she had to do was hang on to her control until she got to Auckland. She wouldn't give him or anyone who worked for him the satisfaction of seeing her break down.

But as she walked across the veranda and down the steps tears blinded her so that she slipped.

He caught her, and she sagged, exhausted. For a moment she was held close to the fierce warmth of his body, locked against the hardness of the muscles she had so lovingly traced only a few hours before. She gave a soft gasp, and looked up into eyes that seared her soul. He was drawn and pale, his mouth tightening into a thin, hard line, but she saw sweat gleam on his skin.

He whispered, 'Damn you, what the hell do you do to me? I'm not going to give in to this madness.'

She pulled herself away. 'An excellent resolution,' she mocked through teeth that wanted to chatter with rage and frustrated desire. 'Then you can sit on top of your little mountain and pretend that nothing can touch you. The great Saul Jerrard, superman, totally in control, so independent that if you touch him he freezes your arm right down to your heart. You look like a human, you even occasionally act like a human, but nothing in this world can convince me that you aren't a robot, programmed to give a damned good imitation of life.'

'You didn't object to my imitation of life last night,' he snarled.

She stared at him. Then she turned away and said evenly, 'I said it was a good imitation. The best, in fact. Your technique is superb, as I'm sure you know. Unfortunately, without a heart, technique and sex-appeal are not worth a tinker's damn.'

It wasn't much of an exit line, but it was all she could manage. All the way down in the car, alone with the taciturn Gil, she stared sightlessly through the windows, refusing to allow herself to feel.

That way lay anguish too deep to be borne. She would have to concentrate on thinking, and eventually, when the pain had eased a little bit, she might be able to contemplate what had happened. In a way she understood his behaviour; she too would have protected Stephanie with her life, but he hadn't needed to show her the way to heaven and then slam the door irretrievably in her face. Last night's self-indulgence was going to cost her dearly in self-respect and happiness. The darker side of paradise, she thought, looking out of the windows at the dramatic mountains and the sea. Cruel gods and mocking legends; the side the tourist publicity didn't mention.

Like a wounded animal she went back to the only place she could call home, but the job she had enjoyed seemed flat and uninteresting, too close to Saul. It was here that she had scoured newspapers and magazines for news of the Jerrards; they were imprinted in the rooms, on the people she saw each day. After a month she gave in her notice, then, when it was worked out she applied for and got a job in the Bay of Islands as a nanny, working for a woman and her husband who ran a big international hotel on one of the islands.

The money was good, although the hours were long, and she wanted a complete change. The two small boys who were her charges were holy terrors, but their need for constant attention kept her mind away from Fala'isi and the pain that lurked at the back of her heart like a dark stain on her life.

She thought she was doing rather well. She still wasn't able to face what had happened to her on Fala'isi, but she was more than content to float along on the surface, her emotions so deeply frozen over that she was beginning to think they'd never thaw out. In a way she hoped they never did. She wasn't exactly enjoying life, but she wasn't suffering either. It was just that her whole existence was grey, without feature or pleasure.

Until one day when her employer said casually to her, 'Don't you think you'd better face the fact that you're pregnant, Candace?'

She bit her lip, appalled at having the secret midnight fear put so bluntly into words. 'Yes, I suppose so. I'm sorry, when I took the job it never occurred to me—just once! How on earth can you get pregnant after just one night?'

'It only takes once—unprotected.' Elizabeth Marshall was briskly sympathetic. 'What are you going to do?'

'I'll work until you get another nanny, of course.'

'I'd ask you to stay, the boys really like you, but I honestly think it would be too much for you. Although I must say you're blooming. I envy women who do that; I always looked like chewed string. Felt like it, too.'

'Well, apart from a few odd physical discomforts I feel wonderful.'

'Yes. You glow. I suppose you don't feel inclined to contact the father?'

Candace shuddered. 'No.'

Elizabeth gave her a quizzical look but nodded, clearly determined not to enquire further. 'In that case, you're going to have to do some hard thinking. There are decisions to be made, and you're the only one who can make them, but if you want to talk it over, feel free. I'll give what help I can.'

Candace had read of women in situations like hers. Hopelessly in love, they were usually ecstatic at the prospect of being pregnant. It would be, they thought, a small piece of the loved one to lavish all their frustrated affections on.

She wondered if she was strange, because all that she could see was a future darker and more bleak than anything she had ever endured. Her whole being rejected the idea of adoption, so that left her with two alternatives. Abortion, or keep the baby and struggle on with the limited sort of life that that would entail.

Abortion? She did not decry it, knew that there were occasions when it was the right, the only solution, but some part of her found it impossible to contemplate. She found herself fiercely protective of the child she carried, seeing it as already a personality, a human being dependent on her for life.

No, abortion was out for her.

That night she walked along the beach in the cool salty air, for the first time deliberately recalling another island, another beach.

She had fallen in love with Saul mindlessly, compulsively, all that was female in her drawn like a moth to the dark flame of his masculinity. And like the moth she had been burned.

But they had made a baby. Oh, she had no doubt that the care of the child would devolve on her, but Saul had participated in the begetting, and he should know about it.

Instantly she pushed the thought to the back of her mind. If she contacted him, he would reject her. She had no proof that the baby was his. And if she was stupid enough to allow him access to the child, would he be tainted with the same blight that infected Saul? Great wealth seemed to eradicate the softer emotions, make those who possessed it remote from the small lives of ordinary people so that they lived on another plane, self-sufficient, ultimately flawed and empty.

Yet was she any better? All her life she had been rejected, until deep in her subconscious she had accepted that that was the normal order of things, that it was her fault.

She no longer believed that, and no one, she decided with cold determination, was going to reject her child. If Saul did refuse to believe that her child was his, then she would force him to accept it. Her child would not be without a father.

It didn't occur to wonder how she knew that he would take his duties as a father seriously.

Clambering up from the gnarled driftwood log where she had been sitting looking listlessly out to sea, she walked back to the hotel, her bare feet making slight indentations by the damp sand. Her mind was made up.

She used directory service to find the London number of the Jerrard organisation, and after dinner that night forced her trembling fingers to dial it. A feminine voice answered, and when she had given her name said calmly, 'Oh, yes, I'll put you through to Mr Jerrard's office, Miss Hume.'

It shouldn't be so easy. 'If he's busy,' she said, suffering second thoughts, 'I'll ring later.'

'No, he gave instructions that you were to be put straight through.'

A click, a pause, and another woman's voice, smooth and cool and efficient, and the same matter-of-fact reaction. Then Saul's voice, abrupt and curt. 'Candace, where the hell are you?'

She winced. 'In New Zealand. Saul, I'm pregnant.'

'Indeed,' he said in a voice smooth as cream. 'Good. Give me your address.'

She gaped, but obeyed, and he said, 'I'll be there within twenty-four hours. Don't move from the place.'

'What do you mean, good? Why is it good?'

'Stephanie sends her love.' And he hung up.

Candace was so enraged that she dialled through again, only to have the cool, calm voice inform her, with a hint of amusement, 'I'm sorry, Miss Hume, but Mr Jerrard has gone. He said to tell you that he'll see you tomorrow, and to take care of yourself.'

'Yes,' she said in a dazed voice.

She was still standing looking at the telephone when Elizabeth came into the room. With relish her employer said, 'I've just had a call from London booking the penthouse for tomorrow night.'

'Oh. Saul.'

The older woman gave her a sharp look. 'Are you all right? You look as though someone hit you on the head.'

'I think I'm all right. I've just rung Saul—the father of the baby. He's coming tomorrow. I think the penthouse is probably for him.'

Elizabeth's brows shot up to her hairline. For once she was shaken out of her hard-won composure. 'Saul Jerrard is your baby's father! How——?' She stopped and bit her lip, looking at Candace as though she had just seen her for the first time, then resumed her normal self-possession with an effort, saying practically, 'I think you did the right thing. And don't worry about the children. Carl's mother is coming tomorrow, and she'll be happy enough to look after them until we find another nanny. You do what you think is the best for you.'

Fine, sensible words. After she had stumbled away to her room Candace stood looking out of the window at the dark mass of the bush in the interior of the island. It lay quiet and still under the moon, as mysterious as the mind of the man she loved. She remembered the last time she had watched a moonrise, the night her baby was conceived. And shivered. What was he planning to do?

*Good.* He had said that her pregnancy was good, but there had been no love in his voice. He had sounded angry, curt, antagonistic. Not loving. Wondering drearily if she was only storing up more pain for herself, she went off to bed at last, to lie staring at the ceiling almost all of the night.

He arrived twenty-five hours after her phone call, in a helicopter, striding from it with the aplomb of a man who was accustomed to being whisked around the world at the crooking of a finger. Candace watched as he was escorted into the hotel; the moonlight gleamed on his hair.

Ten minutes after that her telephone went. 'Come on up,' he commanded smoothly.

# CHAPTER EIGHT

CANDACE was angry with Saul's calm assumption that she would obey, but, after all, she had made the decision to summon him all the way across the world. It was ridiculous to let his arrogance disturb her.

The opulent, elegant hotel was built up a cliff face so that most rooms opened on to the magnificent panorama of the islanded bay. It had very efficient lifts. Two minutes after he had called she was knocking at the penthouse door.

He opened it himself, rolling up the sleeves of his white shirt, his face closed yet sharply alert as he scanned hers for a searing second. 'Come in,' he said, his expression forbidding.

Whatever she had expected, it was not this icy aloofness. She had hoped that his immediate response to her call was indicative of some sort of softening, but she could detect none in the hard bronze mask of his face.

'How are you?' he asked, frowning slightly as she walked past him into the room.

'I'm fine.'

'Have you been to see a doctor?'

She nodded and he said brusquely, 'Well, what did he say?'

She couldn't answer. The penthouse suite came with butler and maid service and she could hear muted sounds from the kitchen as though someone was working there. The mere thought of conducting a conversation like this where it might be overheard made her go cold. She swallowed and asked baldly, 'Why did you come, Saul?'

His mouth curled in a not very pleasant smile. 'To marry you, of course.'

The heated, unspoken hope that had kept her awake all the preceding night died a painful death. Quickly, because it hurt more than anything she had ever done, she said, 'I'm not going to marry you.'

Something ugly moved in the crystalline brilliance of his gaze, but no hint of emotion disturbed the harsh angles and planes of his face. 'Indeed?' he said softly, silkily. 'Had you imagined that it would be so easy, my dear? A meal ticket for the rest of your life, or at least until the baby was sixteen, without the necessity of putting up with me? I'm sorry if you've been spinning little fantasies, but if you want me to support this child you are going to be a hostage. I believe in making sure that every penny I spend works for me.'

The faint unpleasant taste of blood on her tongue convinced her that she had bitten into her lip. Her body geared itself for flight; every hair on her body stood up straight as the sudden surge of adrenalin poured hotly through her veins.

Slowly, carefully, as though she was talking her way out of danger, she said, 'It wouldn't work. You don't love me, and I—and I——'

'And you don't love me,' he finished in a brisk, unemotional tone. 'In my circle, marriages are often made for reasons other than love.'

'I can guess,' she retorted contemptuously. 'To accumulate more money——'

'Or power. To get children.' The words came coldly. 'Well, we've already managed that. What did your doctor say about your health?'

She was pale, but she fought the nausea with courage. 'She said that I was about three and a half months pregnant, that I am slightly underweight, that I need extra iron, but otherwise I'm perfectly healthy.'

His heavy lashes drooped. 'I see,' he said indifferently. 'And you're sure the child is mine.'

She looked around vaguely, found a chair and sat down, conscious of a pain so intense she thought it might burst through her head. 'Yes.'

'I hope you're right.'

'And if it's not?'

'A quick divorce,' he said with a chilling lack of emotion.

He was an alien, someone she had never seen before. He met her stare with a complete lack of interest, his eyes opaque and icy, seemingly uncaring of the pain he was inflicting. In a muted voice she said, 'I can't, Saul. Not like this. I couldn't bear it.'

'Why not?' He came towards her, pulling her up into his arms. She looked up and saw beneath the ice to the flames, more dangerous than ever before because they were banked, held under superhuman control. 'We were damned good in bed. As for anything else, you'll have money, and time. I don't intend to be a particularly demanding husband, nor a mean one.'

His words were like knives in her heart; his mouth bruised and hurt. After a moment he lifted his head, and she saw black frustration and something else, something dark and unknowable in his face, and she shivered.

'I know you want me,' he said harshly. 'Don't make me prove it to you, Candace. I could, if you force me to.'

Her lashes fluttered down. She had thought that being thrown off Fala'isi had been the worst thing that could happen to her. Now she knew that it was not. She could have endured life without him; she was not sure that she could suffer it as his wife.

A knock on the door made her pull away. He let her go to direct the housemaid who stood there, her arms full of what Candace recognised with incredulous anger were her clothes.

'I forgot to organise clothes the last time you spent the night with me,' he said, nothing but a crackle of amusement in his voice when the woman had disappeared into the larger bedroom of the two in the suite. 'I won't be so thoughtless this time.'

Fortunately for Candace's self-control the butler appeared with a tray on which was a bottle of champagne, a frosted pitcher of orange juice and tall, stemmed glasses.

Candace walked across to the window, her thoughts wholly in confusion. With her mind lost in a fog of misery, she needed now the common sense that she had always held to be one of her major attributes.

Well, it had let her down, she thought grimly. Ringing Saul had been one of the bigger mistakes in a life that suddenly seemed littered with them. Turning her head away from the moon-silvered sea outside, she looked across the room to where he stood conferring with the butler, his profile a slash of arrogance against the soft, warm, impersonal ambience of the room. He had no time for softness, no place for it in his life.

She had been right to worry about the effect of vast wealth on her child. It bred soulless automatons, lacking love or charity or compassion.

The butler turned to go, swiftly followed by the housemaid. Without registering the envious look she was given, Candace watched with a leaden heart as Saul picked up a glass of orange juice and one of champagne, and brought them both across.

'There's a small amount of champagne in there,' he said coolly as he gave it to her, 'so it's not likely to hurt the baby. Well, shall we drink to a long and happy marriage?'

'No,' she said, quietly determined. 'I'm not going to marry you.'

'Then I'll take the child from you,' he said. His voice was perfectly calm, his face without expression except for the narrowed slivers of sapphire fire beneath half-lowered lashes. 'In the words of the old cliché, Candace, it's all or nothing. And if I take the baby, there'll be no settlement, no money.'

She tried to find the words to tell him how she despised his shopkeeper attitude, but although the muscles worked her throat had closed up and no words came through. He was watching her with a faint implacable smile and she drew a deep breath and flung the glass of orange juice at him. Most of it missed him, landing on the window behind, but she registered with cold pleasure that some ran down his face.

He continued smiling even while he wiped it from his skin. 'I believe pregnant women often suffer from strange bursts of temperament,' he drawled. 'Or do you just hate losing?'

A note in his voice reduced her to shocked silence. She recognised a savage anger, cold and passionate and menacing.

However, his patronising assumption made her lift her head with a belated attempt at dignity. 'I don't want money, yours or anyone else's. I want a father for my child. I know what it's like to wonder why your father doesn't love you. My child is not going to suffer that. If you're not prepared to accept that I know what I'm doing, you can go back to wherever you came from and I'll tell it you're dead. And I don't like being threatened,' she finished turbulently, because she had told him more than she wanted to about herself.

'Then you'll have to learn to behave.' He poured more champagne, added orange juice and held it out. 'Drink up,' he commanded softly.

She bit her lip, but she took it and drank, and he drank with her, smiling in that cold, uncompromising way that made her fingers itch to slap his face at the same time that it roused her deepest fears.

When she had almost drained the glass she set it down and tried again. 'Saul, marriage would be an awful mistake.'

'Possibly, even probably, but it's going to happen. My child is not going to be born a bastard. I'd have thought you understood the disadvantages of that unhappy situation.' He drank a little more champagne, then set his glass before hers and, before she had time to move away, caught her hand.

Her breath stopped in her throat. She stood very still, her eyes lifted to his face with painful intensity. He applied only the gentlest pressure, his lean fingers imprisoning the fragile bones loosely. Candace heard her heart thunder in her ears as his thumb moved lazily to rest over the pulse beating so quickly beneath the warm ivory of her skin.

'It won't be so bad,' he murmured, his voice deep and lazily caressing. 'And if you marry me you'll be as close to Stephanie as you wanted to be.'

Her lashes fell over agonised eyes. She couldn't bear it, couldn't bear him to use Stephanie as a bribe. The little traitor in her wrist throbbed unmercifully. Her unwilling eyes fell to the darkness of his hand around the pale slenderness of hers. For perhaps the first time in her life she felt frail, totally at the mercy of this man who didn't hesitate to use cruelly ruthless methods to get his own way.

'Let me go,' she said beneath her breath.

As his eyes met hers with lazy insolence he lifted her wrist to his mouth and traced the thin blue vein with the tip of his tongue. A streak of fire shot through her, firing her nerves with torrid anticipation. Sharply, stung to the heart by her untrammelled response, she jerked her hand free.

His laughter was softly mocking. 'So responsive,' he taunted. 'I only have to touch you and your eyes turn smoky and your mouth trembles, and I can see the vibrations sizzling about you like an aura. When I first met your eyes across that restaurant they turned almost black, and I wondered if you were as responsive as they seemed to signify, or if it was a lying delusion, that eager, ardent promise. Yet it was no lie, no fool's paradise, was it, Candace? Whatever you are, however much you hate me, I only have to touch you and you want me almost as much as I want you.'

'I don't hate you, but it's just sex,' she blurted recklessly, almost seduced by the deep note of passion in his voice and her own outrageous need for him.

His head lifted sharply. His expression was shuttered, his mouth a thin line of determination. 'Whatever it is, however bloody troublesome it is, it's more potent than anything I've ever experienced. I know you have nothing to base a comparison on, and I suppose if I had any chivalry at all I'd let you go until you did have, but you are pregnant with my child, and I've just discovered I have very dynastic instincts. I want you more than I've ever wanted any other woman, Candace, and after three and a half months I still want you. Not only that, I haven't wanted another woman since I saw you.'

His words excited her unbearably but she wailed, 'It's not enough for marriage! Sooner or later you'd see another woman you wanted, you'd get tired of me, and I won't have that——'

He gave a feral grin. 'Yes, I remember, you want an ironclad document, that I'll stay around and faithful until the youngest child is off our hands. It will be waiting for us on Fala'isi.'

'I don't!' she shouted, tears spurting shamefully to her eyes. 'I can't think of anything worse than to know that you want to get away and won't because of a stupid contract——'

She was sobbing in real earnest, her face screwed up while she fought for control, her small form shaking as waves of pain racked her.

'Candace,' he said in a shaken voice, and then she was caught and held in an embrace that was wonderfully warm and comforting, in spite of the damp spot where a little of the orange juice had landed on his shirt. 'Hush,' he said as she continued to cry, 'it's all right, it's all right, don't cry any more...'

She couldn't ever remember being held like this and it was sweet, far too sweet, addictively so. Except for the night when they had made love she had never experienced tenderness from him, and this was different, although she didn't know how. Clutching the hard arms that encircled her, she wept into his chest, despising herself and quite unable to stop.

She sobbed, 'We've only known each other three days really.'

'We can court each other after we're married,' he said firmly. 'Candace, please stop, it can't be good for you to cry like this. Don't you like this shirt? First you fling orange juice all over it, now you want to drown it in tears...'

Hiccuping, she groped desperately for a handkerchief, found it and pulled away to blow her nose and wipe her eyes. 'I'm sorry,' she said, low-voiced with humiliation. 'I don't make a habit of—of bawling over—over people.'

'Thank God for that.' He put his hand under her chin and tilted her face for inspection, using his own handkerchief to wipe away the tears that still clung to her lashes. 'I'm sure it's not good for our baby, and it's certainly far too unnerving for me. You've been under some considerable strain, but it's all right now, I'll deal with everything.'

He looked cool, even a little amused, but enough residual tenderness lurked in the depths of his smile to make her swallow her resentment. 'I despise women who weep,' she said firmly.

He nodded. 'Although I believe the latest theories have it that crying is rather good for you.'

She sneaked another look at his face, realising to her astonishment that what she had taken for coldness and withdrawal had been tension overlaid by a remorseless self-control. A wondering, reluctant smile pulled at her mouth. 'I don't see how it can be, it always gives me a stinking headache.'

'In that case, off to bed.' When she hesitated he said, with a return to his previous aloof manner, 'You take the main bedroom, I'll have the other. We must observe the proprieties.' And with enough menace in his voice to send her reluctantly off, 'Goodnight, Candace.'

Once more she lay awake for most of the night, only getting to sleep when the dawn was tinting the sky behind the island. It reminded her very much of the time she had woken up alone in the little house beside the fountain in Fala'isi; again she surfaced to a desolation that ate into her bones and heart, stealing away all delight in the day, rendering it grey and purposeless.

Not that that was anything new. In spite of her best efforts to deny it, when he had thrown her off Fala'isi he had darkened the sunlight in her life. And the reason she had rung him had very little to do with the baby, however hard she had tried to rationalise the decision. She had called him because she was slowly dying without him. It was as simple as that; the baby was just an excuse. She'd had to call him, because she needed him. She, Candace Hume, who had vowed never to need another person as long as she lived, was in love with Saul Jerrard, who was only marrying her because she was pregnant. Not only that, he had become part of the very fabric of her life, a necessity as important as food or water.

It was a terrifying, shattering realisation, one she had fought for as long as she could. Now, lying lonely and sad in her luxurious bed, she took a step further along the path that had perhaps been inevitable since that first exchange of glances across the restaurant at Fala'isi. She admitted that she was going to marry him.

He was up when she finally came out into the sitting-room, speaking crisply into the telephone. She watched him for an unnoticed moment as he said a few curt words. He looked tired, the virile male authority trans-muted to an uncompromising relentlessness. The lines between his brows seemed deeper etched, the mouth held in such a tightly disciplined fashion that it had lost its sensual line.

Then he saw her, and for a millisecond the hardness and self-possession faded, replaced by a naked hunger so acute that she felt it in the pit of her stomach. It vanished instantly, controlled by his formidable will, but her decision had been reinforced.

He might not love her, but whatever he felt for her was strong enough to make it some sort of basis for a marriage. That scorching leap of fire, the possessive, de-manding recognition, had burned through her defences, routing common sense. He had looked, and what he had seen he considered to be his. As she did, she realised. Her love made her just as territorial, just as fiercely de-termined to have him as her mate.

'Yes, immediately,' he said, and hung up.

They surveyed each other with identical carefully blank expressions. In a cotton knit shirt, the lean whipcord lines of his body seemed packed with strength and staying power. He might look tired, but he exuded a male aura that appealed to the most hidden, primitive parts of her.

'Good morning.' He came towards her and took her shoulders, holding her still while he looked down into her face. 'You didn't sleep well.'

'Not particularly.'

He gave a small ironic smile. 'Nor I. Shall we start again, Candace? Will you marry me, without threats and recriminations, so that together we can make some sort of decent life for the child we've made?'

Sudden tears darkened her eyes. She nodded, and he said something under his breath and pulled her into his arms, holding her loosely but with a rocklike strength that she knew now would be hers whenever she felt the need of it.

'I behaved like a swine last night,' he said with his cheek on the top of her head. 'I'm sorry.'

'I was pretty stupid, too. I'm sorry I threw the orange juice over you.'

She could feel his smile. 'It did me the world of good. In spite of drinking gallons of water in the air I always dehydrate while I'm flying.'

It was a small snippet of information, but one she treasured. She wanted to know everything about him. Her finger touched his chest, reacting to the hard, sleek muscle, the faint roughness of his body hair through the thin cotton. 'How did you get here so fast? I know the commercial flights take twenty-seven hours or so, airport to airport, but you were here in much less time than that.'

'The Learjet,' he said succinctly. 'We flew into Kerikeri and a helicopter was waiting. Now, I've decided that we should marry on Fala'isi. Stephanie flew out there yesterday, and is eagerly waiting for us. Can you be ready in an hour?'

She closed her eyes to hide the shadows. Then she nodded. 'Yes,' she said.

'Good.'

He released her, but only to look into her face. She searched his, seeking some sign of tenderness, but there was nothing. He had retreated behind the mask; there was concern in his regard, even a mild affection, but not the hunger she had seen for such a brief second, not a sign of the love her heart craved with such frantic need.

She was marrying Saul Jerrard, billionaire, not the man she had learned to love.

'Perhaps,' he said coolly, 'we should seal that with a kiss.'

It was an open stamp of possession, fierce, passionate, yet oddly impersonal, and when she opened her dazed eyes it was to meet the remoteness of his.

As she turned away to go to the breakfast table she wondered bleakly whether he was showing her without spelling it out that he was not going to allow her to touch him in any way but the most basic. Her place in his life would be that of wife, partner in bed and mother of his child. She would be treated with courtesy and respect, possibly even affection, and the only time they would communicate would be in bed.

She would be a convenience. Like his secretary, and his Learjet, all the other things that existed to save him time and effort. The thought filled her with horror, but by the time she had eaten her first slice of toast she had decided that she would not allow it to be like that. Last night they had communicated; she had jolted him off balance. If that was what it took, then she would do the same again. After all, she had one great ace: the baby.

And she would be seeing Stephanie. A few months ago she would have been ecstatic at the thought of being in constant contact with her half-sister. She thought now with a wry little smile that it was astonishing what falling in love could do to the obsessions of a lifetime.

But Stephanie was a very definite plus.

And so, she thought, watching from beneath her lashes as the man opposite her ate fruit and drank coffee, so are you, my dearest, obstinate, maddeningly self-contained Saul Jerrard.

'Why Fala'isi?' she asked.

He shrugged. 'A marriage there is legal anywhere in the world, and I can control any publicity. And Grant is a distinct plus in getting the documentation done in a hurry. He can be as ruthless as I when it comes to seeing that privacy is maintained. I do not want our wedding turned into a massive media circus.'

She shuddered, thinking of some of the ghastly newspaper reports she had seen. 'No, indeed.'

'As it is,' he said, watching her narrowly, 'there may be comment about the date of the baby's birth. Can you handle it?'

Her shoulders moved in an uneasy shrug. 'Oh, yes, I can handle it. But will anyone dare?'

He smiled, not a pleasant smile. 'A few. Not anyone who wants to stay a friend. I keep as low a profile as possible, but there are always bloodhounds about. And over the years I have made enemies. However, you don't need to worry about them.' Another twist of the thin lips. 'It's amazing what money can do.'

She looked worriedly at him. 'Is the danger for Stephanie all over now?'

'Yes.' A quick sigh of relief was shortened when he continued seriously, 'There are always risks, Candace. All sorts of risks. Not just kidnapping or extortion. I'd be stupid to say the threat of that doesn't exist, but looked at rationally it's pretty minimal. However, there will be people who want to use you for various reasons, either because you will be very rich, or because you will be considered to have some influence on me.'

She nodded. 'I know.'

'I think that's why my family is so important to me. Grant and I are best friends as well as cousins, and I hope you learn to like him and his wife as much as I do. You'll like Tamsyn, anyway. She's a darling, and is a New Zealander like you. Down-to-earth, unpretentious, and kind.'

'Is she?' She looked startled for a moment, before saying in a hopeful voice, 'She sounds nice. Saul, what sort of life will we be living? In spite of all the snooping I did in the gossip columns of the world, I really don't know much about you, what you do, where you live, and quite frankly the thought of living a very social life terrifies me. I'd be bored to screaming-point.'

'And if I said that that was what I wanted?'

The thread of steel in his tone made her pause, but she said almost immediately, 'I'd try, but I'd do my best to convince you that it's a waste of time.'

His laughter was no more than a breath on the sparkling morning air. 'Then it's just as well I have little liking for a social life. I have a circle of friends—not very large, most of whom I've known for a long time. But apart from a few charity events I don't lead a particularly social life. I'm glad you have no hankering to keep up with the jet set because I work too hard to spend much time with them. We'll live near London most of the time, in a small village where Jerrards have been the squires for a couple of hundred years. You will be expected to do the usual things.'

'I don't know what the usual things are,' she objected thinly.

'I'll be able to tell you. I don't do much travelling now—I have delegated most of the responsibility.' His hand came out, gripped hers for a moment. A current of feeling ran through, linking them. In a voice that was deeper than normal, he said, 'I think you'll like living there. The people are ordinary——'

'So am I,' she whispered. 'Very ordinary. Saul, we don't have squires in New Zealand.'

'Yes, you do, it's just not as formalised. You'll be fine. As for ordinary——' Again that almost silent laughter as he got up and drew her into his arms. 'Where on earth did you get that idea?'

She relaxed, allowing the tide of quicksilver to take over. His mouth on her forehead was warm, his arms strong and comforting around her, his body hard, but it was not enough. Still, it was all she was going to get for the moment; she was going to have to learn to be grateful for his kindness.

'I'm not a profoundly social animal,' she said earnestly. 'And all I really want is a family. I'll give it as good a try as I can. If we are patient with each other, surely we'll be able to manage.'

'Patience.' He gave her a sudden dazzling smile. 'It's an old-fashioned virtue, but one I like. Shall we promise to be patient with each other, Candace?'

Suddenly, stupidly shy, she returned his smile. She had the feeling that they had somehow promised each other much more than patience, but the telephone went again, and the moment was lost. Insensibly cheered, she organised herself for the flight to Fala'isi.

It wasn't until they were halfway there, flying in luxury over the wrinkled blue Pacific, that she thought to ask whether Stephanie knew anything.

Saul looked up from the papers that had been waiting for him in the cabin, furnished as an efficient but very comfortable office and conference-room.

'That you are her half-sister?'

She nodded.

'Yes. I told her before I came.'

'What did she say?'

He frowned, whether with impatience or irritation she didn't know. Lean fingers clenched a fraction of a second on the pen he had been using. 'She was astounded, of course, but as soon as she got used to the idea she decided she liked it.'

'Did she know she was adopted?'

'Oh, yes,' he said flatly. 'She knew all the circumstances of her birth, and her parents' deaths, even that her mother committed suicide.'

'I see.' Something struck her. 'Did you know our mother?'

He fitted the top on to the pen. 'Yes,' he said slowly. 'I met her once when I was about fourteen.'

She held her breath. She had spoken to other people who had known her mother, but somehow she wanted to hear Saul's view of her. He knew, too, because before she could ask he said thoughtfully, 'She was a little thing, about your height, and she had something of your attraction, for lack of a better word, a kind of earthy sensuality, completely without artifice, something she didn't understand or even recognise. She was quieter than you are, shy, even a little timorous. I liked her, but I wasn't surprised when I heard that she had committed suicide.'

'She must have been desperate,' she said sadly.

He removed the cap of the pen again. 'I think she was a little unbalanced by my uncle's death. Grief does strange things to people, and even to a fourteen-year-old boy it was plain that she almost worshipped the ground he walked on.'

'When I found out,' she said carefully, 'I couldn't understand how anyone could commit suicide and leave a child behind.'

'Reject Stephanie, as she had rejected you?'

She bit her lip. She shouldn't be astounded by his keen perspicacity, but each new instance of it took her by surprise.

He said very quietly, 'I imagine that she honestly believed that she was doing the right thing for you. I doubt very much whether putting a child for adoption is ever an easy option. And be fair, Candace, most adoptive parents adore their children—your circumstances were tragic and very unusual.'

She nodded. 'I know,' she admitted, 'at least my head knows. I find it a bit difficult to accept with my emotions, that's all.'

Turning away before the conversation became too painful, she pretended to look out of the cabin window, but she could feel his attention on her. Shortly, however, he resumed his work, leaving her to her thoughts, none of them particularly cheerful.

The Learjet came in to land just after sunset on a clear
bright evening; she had wondered whether Stephanie
would be there to meet them, and she was, but with her
were a couple Candace didn't recognise.

'My cousin and his wife,' Saul told her. His mouth
compressed, then relaxed into an unwilling smile. 'They
have suggested that you stay with them until we are
married. Always careful of the proprieties, is Grant.
Perhaps it comes from being brought up by his grand-
mother, a very tough, very conventional old
Frenchwoman.'

He had been like that for the rest of the flight, pleasant
and cool and courteous, as though the morning's flash
of naked desire, and the tenderness that had followed,
had never existed. Or as though he was ashamed of it.

She hoped it wasn't that. Panic of a sort she had never
faced before held her in a particularly fierce grip.

However, she was able to smile and exchange fairly
sensible greetings when she met the Chapmans, a superbly dressed couple, he tall and as dark as Saul with
something of the same air of arrogant strength, his wife
also tall, with a sweet, calm face and magnificent blonde
hair.

Stephanie was exuberant, hugging her brother with
great delight, which faded as she turned to Candace.
Her eyes, so like her brother's, surveyed Candace's carefully collected face. She smiled, and with a similar control
bent to kiss Candace's cheek. 'Hello, sister,' she said
evenly.

Candace kept her smile pinned very firmly on her face.
Scented with that magical aroma of Fala'isi, a perfume
compounded of sea and flowers, a freshness from the
mountains and a faint whiff of coconut, the warm air
flowed like wine around her. She thought she had never
been so miserable in her life.

Something must have warned Saul; his hand slid to
cup her elbow as, in a voice that was indulgent with just

the right amount of concern, he said, 'Come on, we'd better get Candace close to a cup of tea. Flying makes her thirsty and unsettled.'

The Chapmans' house was magnificent, a plantation house built of white blocks of coral limestone, in a garden more formal than that at Saul's house but just as lovely.

Within an hour Candace was tucked up in bed, feeling wretchedly bereft; she had wondered whether Saul would want her in his bed that night, never dreaming for a moment that they wouldn't even be in his house. Tamsyn Chapman had said that it would be easier for her to stay at the plantation as that was where the wedding was being held, and, when it was looked at like that, she was right. But, kind as Tamsyn had been, Candace would have far rather been in Saul's house.

A knock brought her heavy lashes up. Fugitive colour stained her cheeks as she looked across the luxurious room, but it was Stephanie who looked around the carved wooden door.

'Is it all right if I come in?'

'Yes, of course, do, come in and sit down.' She bit her lip to stop her babbling.

'I'm glad you're awake,' Stephanie said, coming in with elaborate quietness and closing the door behind her. 'Saul threatened me with all sorts of horrible things if I woke you, but I had—I had to come in. I wanted to make sure—at least, if Saul says we're sisters, we must be, but it seems so incredible!'

'No.' Candace sat up and held out her hands. 'It's not incredible at all. I came to Fala'isi to look for you.'

Stephanie gave a funny little grimace and came slowly across the room, her expression torn between fascinated interest and a pressing desire to appear adult and in control.

'Sit down,' Candace said, adding crossly, 'I don't know why I'm in bed, I feel fine, just a bit tired, but——'

'But no one says no to Saul.' Stephanie grinned and sat down, looking at her with frank interest. 'And you do look a bit wan and drawn.' She looked down at her skirt and up again, clearing her throat as though it was an effort for her to talk. 'Saul didn't tell me much. He asked me if I remembered you, and for some reason I did, very clearly. I realise now it's because you look like my—our—mother. I've got a few photographs of her.'

'Did you mind?' Candace's voice was husky. Too vividly she recalled Saul's statement, when he had thrown her off the island. Did it hurt Stephanie to know that her birth mother had had an illegitimate child before her?

'No. I might have if I'd known my—our mother, but I don't remember my parents at all, and so, although it was a surprise, it wasn't a great shock, if you know what I mean.'

'I know exactly what you mean,' Candace returned drily.

'I knew I was adopted, of course, and that my birth parents were Mother's brother and his wife, but it never occurred to me that there might be a sister, or other relatives.'

'As far as I know there are none apart from me. Both our mother's parents died fairly soon after she married your father, and as far as I could find out there were no other family, no aunts or uncles still alive. Certainly no close relatives.'

Stephanie looked self-conscious but lifted her head with something of Saul's air. 'What about your adoptive parents?'

'I don't see them any more,' Candace said quietly. She didn't want to talk about them, but Stephanie looked so horrified that she explained, 'Their marriage broke up when I was eight. My father fell in love with another woman, and left us. My mother was shattered. So was I. My father wasn't interested in me—I thought it was because I was adopted. He and his new wife had a baby, and I never saw him again. After a couple of years my mother met another man.'

'And he didn't want you either?'

Candace's smile was mirthless. 'Got it in one. He was a widower, with a family of his own. I was bitterly resentful of his children, but my mother thought he was wonderful. Looking back, I can see that she was the sort of woman who doesn't feel whole unless she has a man. At the time it was no consolation, even if I'd been able to understand her. And I overheard a conversation that—well, never mind. It just served to alienate me even more. All I knew was that no one, not even my own mother, seemed to want me.'

Stephanie said in an appalled voice, 'She didn't, surely, just dump you?'

'No. She tried to smooth things over, she did her best, in spite of what must have been intolerable pressure. But I behaved so badly that in the end everyone, Social Welfare included, decided it would be better for everyone if I was fostered.' Candace gave a tight smile. 'Which actually worked out quite well. At least I knew where I was with foster parents. They were paid to look after you, and they couldn't hurt you.'

'I've never heard of anything so awful in all my life. No wonder you wanted to find out if you had any real family!'

Candace felt wrung out, but Stephanie's anger was heart-warming. This, she hoped, was some sort of breakthrough. Until then, Stephanie had been wary and a little haughty, determined not to give too much away. But the bleak little story had done away with that.

Don't expect everything, Candace warned herself. It's too much to hope for a normal sisterly relationship—whatever that might be! Friendship was all that she could expect to win from Stephanie, and even that would be far more than she had ever expected to attain.

Smiling a little ironically, she said, 'Yes, although I must admit I was horrified when I realised that my half-sister was a part of the well-connected, forbiddingly rich, very powerful Jerrard family. I didn't know whether you knew you were adopted, and when I found out where you were you were only fourteen. So I gave up on the idea of contacting you, deciding to wait out the six years until you were twenty. Only I was interested, of course, and read everything I could about you and Saul, until I'd built up a fairly comprehensive dossier. That's how I knew you had a holiday home here.'

'So you came up here on the off chance?' Stephanie looked intrigued, and a little thrilled, as though the idea of being sought out was not unpleasing.

Candace shrugged. 'No. I knew you were here—I read that you'd been ill and were convalescing.'

'Glandular fever,' Stephanie told her grimly. 'A nasty bout, believe me.'

'Are you all right now?'

'Oh, fully recovered. And then we met, in the market. Or had you been following us?'

Candace laughed. 'I'd seen your brother and the red—Lydia Woolcott—at a restaurant the night before, but no, I wasn't following you. That meeting was sheer luck.'

'And you fainted, right in front of us!'

'That,' Candace said cautiously, 'was not luck. Or the heat.'

## CHAPTER NINE

STEPHANIE gave a gurgle of laughter. 'Really? How clever of you! I was completely taken in.'

Not aware of exactly what Saul had told Stephanie, Candace decided to ignore the fact that her faint had not fooled anyone else.

'I admired you that day,' Stephanie told her. 'Lydia behaved so badly, doing her bored sophisticate act all over the place, and you smiled and gave her as good as you got. Oh, she was such a nuisance! I was so glad when Saul sent her home. She spent all her time oozing around, slithering all over Saul, and she had the coldest eyes of anyone I've ever met. I don't know what Saul was thinking of, bringing her out here.'

'I've heard,' Candace said angrily, betrayed into indiscretion because she knew why Saul had brought Lydia, and she didn't like it one bit, 'that tycoons usually get their kicks from power, not sex. So perhaps one woman is much like another.'

Stephanie gave a shocked little gasp. 'Oh, I'm sorry, I shouldn't have gone burbling on about—I mean, I don't think they were—they were—— Well, she looked *hungry*, if you understand what I mean!' Trying very hard to regain some poise, she subsided into silence, looking somewhat anxiously over at Candace.

Who had her own apologies to make. 'I'm sorry, too, that was cheap and untrue.'

'Well, they say love makes you awfully jealous,' Stephanie said knowledgeably. 'And I should think anyone might be jealous of Lydia—because she's superb-looking, isn't she?—but quite frankly I don't think Saul was taken in by her one bit. In spite of all her clever conversation she's a stupid woman—you couldn't discuss

173

anything with her, not really. And Saul is awfully clever.'
Her anxious look intensified. Taking a deep breath, she
said swiftly, 'This is the most awful cheek, but you do
love him, don't you?'

Candace nodded. 'I'd die for him,' she said shakily.

'He needs someone to love him like that.' Stephanie
hesitated again. 'He's been so good to me, I want him
to be happy. He can be stuffy and tough, and, try as
hard as I can, I can't coax or persuade or wheedle him
into letting me do anything he doesn't want me to, and
he has totally archaic ideas of what is suitable for his
sister, but he's always there for me when I need him,
and I think that's truly vital, don't you?'

Candace, who knew only too well what it was like to
have the secure foundations of her life eroded, nodded
soberly. Yes, Stephanie was right. Saul always would be
there, both for their child and for her. What right had
she to cry for the moon when she could have that?

'I think you'll be good for him,' Stephanie went on,
in full flow. 'Sometimes he seems to be—distant, as
though he's gone somewhere a long way away. It's because he has such awful responsibilities and has to make
really stressful decisions. He needs warmth, and someone
who loves him, not the material things he can give her.
I liked you right from the start, even though I thought
you might be using me to get to Saul.'

Candace flinched. 'You too?'

'Oh, it happens—used to happen!—all the time. All
my friends at school and their older sisters think he's
absolutely wonderful, and they make a big play for me
so I'll invite them home for the holidays.' She didn't
seem overly worried. Indeed, a wicked grin spread over
her face. 'They will,' she finished with great satisfaction, 'be absolutely furious when word of this gets
out.'

A sinking feeling in Candace's stomach robbed the
reunion of some of its excitement. She couldn't, however,
say anything to Stephanie. When at last the younger

woman left, apparently completely reconciled to her newly discovered sister, Candace lay back and wondered just what she was going to do as Saul's wife. If he loved her, then they would be able to make some sort of satisfactory life together, even though she knew nothing about the circles he moved in. But he didn't love her, and she had no idea of how he expected her to behave. What sort of life would she lead? Left to care for his child while he lost himself in business affairs?

Restlessness impelled her from the bed across to the graceful french windows. For a long time she stood looking out through a haze of silk gauze to the moonlit scene beyond. The quiet chuckle of a fountain brought back vivid memories of the night when she had found paradise in Saul's arms. She touched her waist, smiling a little tigerishly. Was she sorry?

Yes—and no. She hadn't wanted a baby, but now that she and Saul had made one, she already loved it with a fundamental protective affection. And, although she had every right to be apprehensive about her future as Saul's wife, some deep vein of optimism comforted her.

At least they had a matching sensual need for each other. Or was it always like that for a man? She was too inexperienced to know. What had seemed incredible rapture to her could have been just the usual thing for him. No doubt Lydia would be able to tell the difference between everyday sex and raging passion, she thought caustically.

Bed had never seemed so undesirable. She stepped through the wide door on to a terrace. Further on, the damp, close-cut grass of the lawn was cool and soothing on her bare feet. Her nightgown swirled gently around her ankles, the thin white cotton cool on her hot skin, her narrow brows drawn together in a frown.

Under no illusions about Saul's character, she recognised that he could make her so wretched that the unhappy years of her childhood would seem like a picnic by comparison. If only she didn't love him so...

But at least Stephanie seemed disposed to be friendly. She gave a small reminiscent smile. Even if they never learned to love one another, she thought they would eventually settle into a steadfast affection. Oh, she hoped so. It would break her heart if her sister disliked her.

Her sixth sense warning her of his noiseless approach, she turned and watched him come across the wet grass, the moon striking dark fire from his hair. A stark pang of need ripped through her; she managed to hide it by clasping her hands together in front of her and standing very straight and still.

His voice was brusque as he came to a stop before her, so that she looked up into a face carved in stone. 'What are you doing out here?'

'I couldn't sleep.'

'I see. Grant and I have just finished a session in the library, and I was on my way to bed when I saw you flitting like a wraith across the garden. What's worrying you?'

'I think I might be making the biggest mistake I've ever made, in a career scattered with them.'

Something hardened in his face but his voice remained the same, level, almost amused. 'Do you? I thought it was men who were supposed to be reluctant.'

'Aren't you?'

His shoulders moved in a shrug. 'Oddly enough, no. I think we can make a good life together, and I want my child.'

In spite of his threats it seemed he had no doubts about the parentage of his baby. Something eased inside Candace, some hard little knot of pain. It emboldened her to whisper, 'Saul,' as his mouth found the exquisitely sensitive hollow behind her ear.

His breath was erotically warm on her skin. 'I didn't come here for that,' he muttered.

She shivered. 'Then why did you come?'

'I wanted to make sure you were all right and give you this.'

He reached into his pocket and pulled out a cascade of dark moonlight. The pearls were warm with the heat of his body, the diamond clasp glittering with a cold fire that contrasted brilliantly with their smooth glow.

Candace stood still while he fastened the three magnificent strings around her throat, her eyes so heavily weighted that they were almost closed.

'I thought they would suit you,' he murmured.

'Are they from the island?'

'Yes, Fala'isi's black pearls. Some were my mother's dowry, others I've collected over the years. I must have known that some day I'd find a woman with the skin and eyes to suit these dark ones.' He smiled. 'Tamsyn has the Chapman string, pale as a dove's breast; they suit her blonde beauty, but these are made for you.'

'Like the moonlight on the pool at the house...'

He nodded. 'Yes. I thought of that, too. At the house where we made love.'

Her finger lingered over them. Suddenly, with a flame of that newly discovered rashness, she found the courage to take the biggest gamble of her life. 'Saul, I love you. If you can't love me I'd rather you called the wedding off. If you do, I won't hide the baby from you, or put any obstacles in the way of your seeing as much of it as you want to. It will be cruel of you to marry me if you don't—can't love me in return.'

He was very still, his narrowed eyes gleaming like black sapphires in the darkness. Then he expelled a sharp breath and said harshly, 'Always the unexpected. And so naïve. Don't you know, you idiot, that I fell head over heels in love with you the first time I saw you?'

Astonishment kept her silent. She began to shake, as much from the sudden and great release of tension as from joy, and turned her face blindly into his shoulder.

'Why didn't you tell me, you bastard?' she whispered on a sob. 'I've been so miserable.'

'Hush, my dearest heart. I've been just as miserable, and when I'm angry I have this rotten habit of making sure that everyone suffers with me, especially the person who's causing the pain.'

His arms tightened. They stood for long moments clasped together, until he loosened his hold and tipped her head back. Tears tracked down the smooth skin of her cheeks; he swore in a muffled voice and picked her up in a smooth, unexpected movement. 'My poor love, you're worn out and I'm a sadist for inflicting this——'

She kissed his jaw. 'I'm not worn out, I've never felt better in my life, and I'm certainly not your poor love, I'm not a poor anything! If you love me, I'm the richest woman in the world.'

'No, no, that's an exaggeration. There are quite a few——'

She choked with laughter, astounded that he could joke about something that had loomed large enough to assume mountainous proportions in her mind. 'I'm rich because you love me,' she said softly. 'If you didn't have a penny, I'd still be the richest person in the world. And quite frankly, I'd just as soon you didn't have so much disgusting money. I really am nervous about the sort of life we'll live after we're married—it would be nice if you were a struggling worker. Then I could help you.'

They had reached her windows. He pushed through the billowing silk and strode across to deposit her on the bed. Then he leaned over and gave her a firm, but not sensuous kiss. 'You will help me,' he promised deeply, his intonation making the words a vow and a promise, 'by being you, the woman I fell in love with, the only woman who has ever touched my cold heart. That's all I want from you, your presence in my life from now on. We'll worry about anything else afterwards, and we'll make a life that suits us both, and Stephanie, and our children. Now, go to sleep. Tamsyn has a fairly busy schedule mapped out for you. At the top of the list is a wedding dress.'

She gave a horrified start. 'I never thought—I don't
need a proper wedding dress——'

'Why? It's going to be a proper wedding.'

Sudden stupid tears filtered through her lashes. 'I
know,' she whispered, pressing a kiss to the hand that
smoothed a thick silken lock from her brow.

In a voice that was wonderfully tender in spite of an
underlying tension, he said, 'You need to get some sleep.
If the flight hasn't tired you all this unbridled emotion
definitely has. Dearest heart, we have all of our lives
ahead of us. I can give you this night of uninterrupted
rest.'

She gave him a misty smile and settled down, watching
adoringly as he walked away. He was almost out of the
room when she gave a gasp and sat up. 'Saul, the pearls!
You'd better take them with you.'

'No. They're yours.'

She wore them, dark gleam of moonlight around her
throat, against a dress the clear sunlit grey of her eyes,
a silk dream of a dress that had been miraculously
whipped up by a svelte American woman who owned a
boutique in the town. She wore them with a smile so
radiant it made everyone who saw her sigh romantically.
She wore them with incandescent happiness and complete trust in the man she was going to marry.

The ceremony was held in the small cathedral in the
town, the congregation mainly islanders who packed the
pews to see the man they called one of their own married,
their magnificent harmonies blending in anthems of
praise that were dim echoes of the emotions in Candace's
heart.

She had asked, with careful caution, Stephanie to be
bridesmaid. And received her first hug from her sister.

'Lovely, I've always wanted to be a bridesmaid, thank
you, thank you, thank you!'

Radiant in her best blue silk dress, she made an exceptionally pretty attendant, one who was determined
that everything should be done exactly right. It was she

who insisted that Candace wear for her 'something old'
a seed pearl and garnet bracelet that had been their
mother's. Aching with pride and love, Candace wore it,
and knew joy and acceptance.

Grant was best man, while Tamsyn, as she said later,
made a very good mother of the bride, even to the point
of crying cheerfully at the right times. Their three
children, two girls and a boy who was going to be his
father all over again, had been reserved with Candace
at first, but soon accepted her. As well as the joy of his
love, and this marriage, Saul was giving her a family.

And she would give them all up, except perhaps
Stephanie, she thought as she walked down the aisle,
pale pink and green orchids in her hands, for the man
who waited for her at the altar.

Her hands trembled. She had chosen to walk down
the aisle with only Stephanie in attendance, and it suddenly seemed a long, lonely trek towards a future that
could not possibly live up to her high hopes. Every lesson
she had learned in her life seemed to dance in front of
her, hideous mockeries warning her that eventually he
too would reject her, who was she to hope for——?

At that moment Saul turned his head. As though he
understood, his strong, beautifully moulded mouth
curved in the smallest of smiles, tenderly reassuring, and
all the phantoms shrivelled and died. She straightened,
the orchids that had been quivering became steady, as
steady as her voice when she made her vows.

Afterwards, while the church bells rang and the tourists
in the streets turned to watch the wedding cars as they
took them back to the Chapmans' house, she sat with
the man she had promised to love and honour all her
life, her hand clasped in his. Even through the darkened
glass of the windows the sun caught the gleam of her
wedding ring.

He lifted her hand and kissed the ring, and her palm.
'I thought you were going to run,' he said quietly.

'It was so stupid—I lost my nerve.'

His hand tightened. 'I would have followed you if you'd run across the universe. But I'm glad I didn't have to.'

The wedding reception was small and informal, followed by a visit to the big celebration held at the village close by the house, which was much more formal, and conducted almost entirely in the lovely liquid sounds of the Fala'isian language, which Saul spoke fluently.

But when that was over, and they had been sped on their way with advice that made everyone laugh and the old, old woman who had given it had winked at Candace and whispered, 'Don't need to tell him, he was born knowing how to make a woman happy,' they were at last alone, heading along a road she recognised.

'What did she say?' she asked demurely, feasting her eyes on his profile, remembering the turmoil of her feelings the last time he had driven her along this route.

His grin was free and unforced. 'If you want to make a woman happy, beat her when she needs it, love her, and never stop telling her she is beautiful. But above all, keep her nights busy as well as her days.'

'And the last little bit, the part she whispered so softly only you and she could hear?'

His smile narrowed. 'She said that I was lucky, it is not every woman who gives her man a son the first time.'

Colour flooded her skin. 'How did she know?'

'I suppose she's seen many pregnant women. As for the baby's sex—certain older women among the islanders seem to have the talent for predicting it.'

'How accurate are they?'

He laughed. 'About eighty per cent, but don't worry about it. Daughter or son, our baby will be loved.'

She nodded, her hand skimming her waist, her heart full. There had been a note of such satisfaction in his voice that she felt like weeping. However, another thought struck her. 'Do you think anyone else suspected?' she asked worriedly.

'No, why should they? Perhaps Tamsyn. She's been very solicitous of you. Does the prospect embarrass you?'

'I suppose it does,' she said quietly. 'You too, or you'd have told Grant.'

His shoulders moved slightly. 'No. I want any fuss about our marriage to have died down a little before you have to face any questions about a pregnancy.' He took his eyes off the road for a moment to scan her subdued face. 'What is it, my heart?' he asked softly.

She gave him a constricted smile. 'I suppose I need reassurance, or something. I'm just being stupid. And I feel that I should have contacted my adoptive parents.'

'Are you sure?' His tone was completely non-committal.

She nodded slowly, frowning a little. 'Yes. I've spent so many years hating them, I'd like to make an end of all the resentment and the unhappiness and the pain. I don't expect anything from them any longer, so they can't hurt me, and I think my mother, anyway, would like to know that everything has worked out so—so idyllically for me.'

She had told him about that incident when her mother had forced money on her; looking back now Candace cringed at her own younger, self-righteous self, stiff with years of prejudice and alienation.

'I'm so happy now,' she finished, 'I'd like them to know that in a way I understand why they behaved how they did.'

'You must do whatever you feel is right,' he said calmly.

In a way it was like an epilogue to her life, a tidying-up of loose ends. She let go of all the turmoil and pain, for the first time able to relax in the joyous certainty of her happiness.

It was dusk, a radiant glowing dusk, when he picked her up and carried her across the threshold of the little house high in the mountains, his face for once unguarded and open, his compelling features irradiated by a happiness she had put there.

He set her down, sliding her the length of his body, and kissed her. 'Welcome home, my heart.'

It was sweet and slow, a promise and a commitment; then they went together into the drawing-room. Obviously someone had prepared the house for them; gardenias scented the air, and champagne rested in a silver bucket beside two tall flutes.

Still clad in the moondress and pearls, Candace walked across to stand in the open french window and gaze out across the pools. The water-lilies were closing, their pale flowers gleaming like promises in the darkness. A strange emotion held her in thrall, a combination of excitement and melancholy.

Tiredness, she told herself, her hand touching her waist. Her skin registered his approach, but she didn't turn.

'You look sad,' he said quietly.

She lifted her face in a startled little movement. Whatever she had expected him to say, it wasn't that.

On a half-drawn breath, she said, 'I feel—odd. As if I'm standing on the edge of a precipice, with no place to go but over.'

'Why?'

She had never thought that she would tell anyone, not even this man she loved with everything that was in her, but something forced the words from her. Still not looking at him, not touching, she said almost defensively, 'I've always been terrified of loving, of wanting. I grew up convinced that loving anyone was a fast way to total lack of control.' At last she turned, looked up into his lean, impassive face. 'I'm afraid, Saul.'

'That if you let yourself, you'll be as lost to desire as your parents.'

She nodded. 'I'm afraid,' she repeated in a whisper.

The slashing lines of his face tautened. 'Me too. Do you think I wanted to fall in love with you? You could have been a terrorist, or a cheap opportunist, yet before I knew it I was in thrall to this damned hunger. I thought, God, you're falling for her, you fool, and I hated myself. How the hell could I fall in love with a woman like you, with secrets in your eyes?'

Candace slid her arms around his waist, holding him tight, her uplifted face dismayed. He was taut and stiff in her embrace, but almost immediately the savagery in his expression faded, and he touched her cheek with a curved hand, gently, with infinite possession.

'You were so sweet and ripe and fiery, with your soft red mouth and your hair like amber silk; you looked at me with a kind of shock, and my whole body ached with the need to take you. I was appalled. I deliberately encouraged myself to think the worst. I wanted you to be someone who was evil and vicious, so that I could make you suffer because I was falling in love with you.'

His arms tightened about her. 'I toyed with the idea of keeping you imprisoned here, using the elemental attraction between us to get you into bed, then slake myself in you until the sight of you sickened me. But you didn't seem to be experienced; not even a hardened criminal can blush to order. I told myself that even terrorists have some sort of moral code, often quite rigid, and that Stephanie's safety was of paramount importance, so vital that it justified any means I had to take to protect it.'

His eyes darkened as he rested his cheek on the top of her head. 'But I found I couldn't just take you, without respect or care.'

In a very small voice, she said, 'I thought that was what you had done when you threw me out. After we'd made love.'

His face hardened into lines of self-contempt. 'I couldn't believe it had happened to me. There have been other women, not as many as the gossip columns have it, but some, and, although I'd enjoyed making love with them, it was nothing like the explosion of the senses we shared. You were silky and fiery and responsive, honest and ardent and giving, and I knew I was lost. But you were also Stephanie's half-sister; that was why you had gone out with me, come to my home, smiled at me and made me laugh—it was all because you wanted to get in touch with Stephanie. I was in total confusion——' He stopped and kissed her, brutally, with such passion that she welcomed the hard voracity of his mouth.

'I knew then that I loved you,' she whispered against his lips. 'I was confused too, because you'd been so cold and self-controlled, and then we made love and it was like being burned to death by desire. Total loss of self-control. All my silly complexes surged to the fore. But why did you offer me money?'

His mouth twisted. 'I managed to convince myself that you had slept with me to make sure of meeting Stephanie again.'

'A somewhat extreme method of keeping in touch, wouldn't you say?' Her voice was very dry, and he gave a soft laugh.

'My dearest love, by then I'd known what it was like to lie in your arms, be welcomed into your body and consumed by the fire there. Extreme describes my re-action fairly well! I offered you money, and you threw it in my face, which was the response I'd been hoping for.'

'Then why——?'

He gave her a twisted, derisory smile. 'I told you I was confused! Making love to you had been like finding the Grail, touching the rainbow, walking in through the gates of paradise, everything I had wanted and never expected to find, yet I was overcome with remorse. You'd been a virgin, and, although I still hadn't accepted that marriage was the only solution for you and me, I fan-tasised about chaining you to me for the rest of your life. But I needed time to think, time spent away from the fire in my blood whenever I looked at you, and I think you needed that, also. Was I right?'

Reluctantly, her eyes shadowed as she recalled the weeks spent away from him, she nodded. 'Yes, but oh, I missed you. I wanted to die.'

'Yes,' he said. His mouth twisted, and she caught a glimpse of remembered hell in the blazing eyes. 'Oh, I didn't give in easily. I looked at some of the most beautiful women in the world, and didn't want one. When I realised that it was only a matter of time before I gave in and came crawling back, it was a bitter discovery.'

She made a soft sound of dismay and he smiled without humour. 'Amusing, isn't it? I'm not a particularly pleasant character, Candace. If you'd wanted a Prince Charming you should have found another man. My emotions are violent.'

'So are mine,' she admitted. 'I think that is one of the reasons that I'm afraid. Of losing control. Of being less than I am.'

'It happens to all of us,' he said softly, kissing her lashes closed, his mouth unbearably gentle. 'Why did you let me know that you were pregnant?'

'The baby is part of you. You have a right to know. And it has a right to know its father. But I rang you because I was dying without you.'

He nodded, his mouth tracing the line of her brows, soft as a dove's feather. It set tiny thrills of sensation quivering through her body from the sensitive nerves in her mouth and the back of her neck to her loins. 'I know, dear heart. I was delighted when you rang. I thought that at last I could claim you without losing face. My damnable pride! And then I arrived, and you told me bluntly that you weren't going to marry me.' He kissed her, harshly, brutally, then with exquisite care. 'I went mad. I had never felt such—such fury, such pain. All I could think of was that I loved you and wanted you with total passion, and you didn't feel the same as me. I wanted to hurt you as much as I was hurting. I wasn't sane.'

She shivered, remembering the bleak pragmatism with which he had set their marriage plans in action. 'I did love you,' she said into his chest. 'Only I didn't think you could love me. I didn't think you could love anyone. I had such stupid ideas—I thought that because you are indecently rich it meant that you were different——'

'But I'm a man, Candace. I bleed when I'm cut.'

She nodded, shamefaced. 'Yes. I was trying to hurt you.'

'You did, but you had every right. I had just taken the most wonderful experience of my life and, because I was afraid, I turned it into dross. I deserved to suffer a little.' He kissed her again, a slow, sweet kiss that made her heart thump in her throat.

When it was over she leaned against him, saying deeply, 'How can you be so convinced that women chase you just for your money? You must know that you're the most astonishingly handsome man I've ever seen. In fact, I resented you so much because you seemed to have everything—the kind of character that marks you out from the common herd, physical perfection, and an inordinate amount of the world's wealth. How can you love me? I'm no prettier than millions of women, I lied to you, I used——'

'You are beautiful, but even if you weren't I'd still love you. I don't know, I looked at you across a restaurant, and something basic, completely fundamental happened, like a rearrangement of cells. I was translated into a different state. I wasn't the same man. It happened for you, too, didn't it?'

She nodded. 'Yes. I thought it was fear, because I knew I was going to try to contact Stephanie, but I suppose I knew that it was something much more dangerous. I kept telling myself that I was being stupid. I was sure that, whatever it was, it wasn't going to last.'

'I tried that, too,' he said grimly. 'But the more I convinced myself that as soon as I'd had you this damned inconvenient passion would be sated, the more I knew

I was fooling myself. Which doesn't excuse, although it might explain, my brutal behaviour towards you.'

Outside the moon emerged from behind a cloud, bathing the gardens in a flood of exquisite golden light. As if answering a cue, the sweet, bell tones of the tikau's call floated on the scented air, evocative of other lovers who had been given their heart's desire.

He must have sensed her silent recognition, because he said on a soft laugh, 'I should have known, the first time we heard it, that I'd had my chips. Damned legend...'

'I thought it was like all legends, giving me my heart's desire, yet preventing me from ever achieving what I wanted so badly.'

He tipped her head back, his incredible eyes banked, the hard mouth softened by a wonderfully tender smile. 'Fools, both of us.'

She nodded, then gasped as his strong arms lifted her free of the floor. He said insinuatingly, 'Darling, I'm just taking you to bed. I'm sure you must be exhausted after that display of unbridled emotion. You need a rest.'

'And you?' she asked solemnly. 'Do you need a rest too?'

He kicked open the door into the bedroom with one elegantly shod foot. 'I've been indulging in unbridled emotion too. Yes, I think I need a few hours spent in bed.'

This time it was slow and all-consuming, a leisurely, passionate exploration that sent them soaring out beyond the confines of the earth, yet somehow made the bedroom the centre and sum of the universe, narrowing down space and time until all Candace was aware of was the joyous desire that ached through her body, and his restrained, slow response, patient, wildly exciting, completely controlled.

But at last, when he had reduced her to a sensual being, sobbing her ardour in his arms, ah, then he too became lost in sensation, calling her name in ecstasy as he spilled

his essence into her, sating her, sending her rocketing
off into some other realm where she was transported by
delight, her bones fire and honey, her mouth filled with
his taste, her nostrils with his scent, her heart with his
love.

'I think,' he said aeons later, when they had slept and
woken in each other's arms, 'that, as in all the best
legends, happy ever after was made for us.'

'Mmm,' She felt his laughter lift his chest and put out
her hand, smoothing through the fine scrolls with a
languid finger.

'Not that I'm superstitious, mind you.'

She chuckled. 'Oh, no. Not in the least.'

In a deepening voice, he said, 'I thank whatever gods
there are for bringing you to me. I love you, Candace.'

The simple avowal was all that she needed. She lifted
her face and kissed him sweetly. 'I love you too.'

'I know.'

An even simpler response, but one that satisfied her
completely. She knew that whatever happened in the
future their love and trust were now strong enough to
survive anything. In the best way of all. They knew each
other and that knowing would support them through
their life together. Here, in this closest place to paradise,
they had been shown the darker side of it. From now
on they would live in a paradise of their own making.

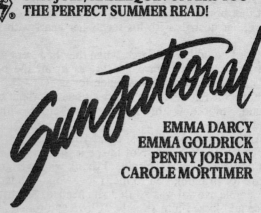

**Back by Popular Demand**

# Janet Dailey
## Americana

A romantic tour of America through fifty favorite Harlequin Presents, each set in a different state researched by Janet and her husband, Bill. A journey of a lifetime in one cherished collection.

In August, don't miss the exciting states featured in:

**Title #13 — ILLINOIS**
     **The Lyon's Share**

  **#14 — INDIANA**
     **The Indy Man**

### *Available wherever*
### *Harlequin books are sold.*

# Take 4 bestselling love stories FREE

## Plus get a FREE surprise gift!

This August, don't miss an exclusive
two-in-one collection of earlier love stories

# MAN
# WITH A PAST

---

# TRUE COLORS

### by one of today's hottest
### romance authors,

*Jayne Ann Krentz*

Now, two of Jayne Ann Krentz's most loved books are
available together in this special edition that new and
longtime fans will want to add to their bookshelves.

Let Jayne Ann Krentz capture your hearts with the love
stories, MAN WITH A PAST and TRUE COLORS.

And in October, watch for the second two-in-one
collection by Barbara Delinsky!

Available wherever Harlequin books are sold.

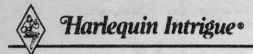

# Trust No One...

When you are outwitting a cunning killer, confronting dark secrets or unmasking a devious imposter, it's hard to know whom to trust. Strong arms reach out to embrace you—but are they a safe harbor...or a tiger's den?

When you're on the run, do you dare to fall in love?

For heart-stopping suspense and heart-stirring romance, read Harlequin Intrigue. Two new titles each month.

## HARLEQUIN INTRIGUE—where you can expect the unexpected.